# THE BEAST OF DEVIL'S ROCK

## MICHAEL COLE

SEVERED PRESS
HOBART TASMANIA

# THE BEAST OF DEVIL'S ROCK

Copyright © 2019 Michael Cole

*WWW.SEVEREDPRESS.COM*

*ISBN: 978-1-925840-94-0*

# CHAPTER 1

The air was white with a thousand streaks as the wind carried the heavy snow horizontally across the Krisha Forest. The sky was a dim twilight, shining grey streams of sunshine across the atmosphere as it neared sunset. Pines and firs, their green color obscured under white powder, twisted and rocked like angry protesters as the wind tore through the forest. As it gusted between them, the wind took on an eerie howl, as though it were a chorus from countless angry spirits hidden beneath the canopy.

In the gap between these trees was the main road, the cracked grey pavement covered in snow and ice. Like a huge artery system, the road stretched across the county, with smaller side roads branching from it deep into the forest. As would be typical during such a storm, these roads were near vacant, save for one Ford Interceptor stuck against a snowbank. Its dark blue paint was invisible as snow caked the hood and doors. Its black tires were almost just as indiscernible, despite the efforts of the Sheriff's Deputy attempting to dig around them.

Corporal Ron Weller cringed yet again from the icy sting. The Beeman County Sheriff's Deputy muttered numerous curse words, each one visible as hot breath in the cold January air. He swore the snow was specifically aiming for the small open space between his coat collar and hat. And its aim was accurate, which prompted him to scrunch his shoulders up to keep the flakes from hitting his skin. The Beeman County Sheriff Department provided hoods that snapped to the back of the jackets. Weller usually didn't wear them, as he didn't like how they pulled on the collar when they hung back. He was regretting not wearing one now, about as much as he regretted taking on this assignment.

He leaned down, holding his breath to avoid breathing in the exhaust that wafted from the tail pipe. With both hands on the ice scraper, he scraped away at the snow that bunched at the rear passenger tire. Laying in the snow beside his boots was the broken wood handle to a snow shovel, which had snapped near the base.

The police Ford Interceptor was stuck against a snowbank, a consequence of spiraling out. The remaining handle near the scoop was barely the length of a popsicle stick, which gave him little-to-no leverage in digging out the snow. The ice scraper was holding up so far, though he was careful not to scoop too much at a time in order to avoid snapping it also. He just needed to get enough of the compressed snow away from the tires to allow the vehicle enough traction to get moving again.

Another large flake zipped under his collar like a meteor, landing firmly on the skin. Weller arched and staggered back as though struck by a bolt of lightning.

"Son-of-a--!" he called out.

The driver's side window rolled down. Deputy Charles Pat stuck his rounded head out and looked back at him.

"You good?"

Weller watched as Pat waved his hand over his face to defend against the steady assault of snowflakes. The heater was on full blast, sending hot air escaping through the window like steam from a spa.

"Oh, me?" Weller said. "I'm just dandy. It's you I'm worried about. Hate to have you overheat in there."

"Hey, you volunteered," Pat quipped.

"Yes, I did," Weller said. *Just one more out of a bunch of stupid decisions.*

"Sure you don't want me to radio it in?"

"No, I think I just about got it."

"You said that last time."

"Hey, you're more than welcome to give it a try."

Pat nodded as though in agreement. "You know? I think I'm good." Pat disappeared back into the vehicle and rolled the window back up.

"Figured as much, you pudgy bastard," Weller muttered. He continued scraping away at the snow. He hoped he was right about almost being dug out. There were two reasons he didn't want to inform Dispatch that they were stuck. One was the fact that it would take hours for anyone to get out there. The county had all of its plows in the central town areas. Outskirt areas were always the last to be plowed, if ever, by the county. The main road was usually plowed by a private contractor, if he wasn't hired out by the

County first. The second reason was the fact that it was just plain too embarrassing. The other officers would be relentless in making Weller and Pat the butt of a hundred jokes. Weller would rather do without it.

He reached in with his left leg and scraped his boot against the side of the tire, knocking some of the snow away from the treads. It piled up around his heels as he brushed it back. That was the one good decision he did make; wearing muck boots. He knew the snow would soak his regular boots, one of the reasons Pat was more than enthusiastic to stay inside.

With about two inches dug out from around the tires, Weller stepped around to the driver's side window. He tapped on the glass to get Pat's attention.

"Okay, give it a try."

Pat put the vehicle in forward gear and stepped on the accelerator. The tires spun and the vehicle inched forward. It struggled a brief moment as it cleared the dug-out space. But with enough momentum, it continued forward.

Pat rolled down the window. "Sweet!"

"Finally!" Weller said. It was a heartfelt sentiment, as he was eager to get out of this weather. Even under his insulated gloves, his fingers felt frozen from digging the frozen mounds. The wind was relentless. Moreover, Weller hated listening to the endless whistle within the trees. The branches were in constant movement, like beasts clashing against each other. The lack of sunlight only made it more ominous. He collected the broken pieces of the snow shovel and tossed them into the trunk. He brushed the snow off his body then threw himself into the passenger seat.

"Is it chilly out there?" Pat joked.

"You know, you should've been the one to do the digging. Not like you're lacking in insulation," Weller said.

"Ha! Funny. Fat joke!" Pat said. He grinned, not taking genuine offense as it was a constant subject of their banter. He put the vehicle in reverse and backtracked over their path to gain a little extra traction. With the Interceptor back in forward gear, he cut over the snow, flooring the pedal to get over the initial lump. The Interceptor bumped as it gained enough traction to move through the snow.

"Holy crap, Charlie, be careful," Weller said. "I really don't feel like spinning out again."

"Hey, if I didn't we'd be stuck again for sure, the way this shit is coming down. Unless you'd prefer I didn't stop to let you in?"

Weller shook his head and watched the endless streams of snow descending onto the road.

"Where the hell is Matt? As long as we've been out here, you think we would've passed him at least once."

"Maybe he's plowing back in town," Pat said.

"He'd've gone back that way," Weller said, pointing behind them with his thumb. "Knowing him, he'd've had the plow down on his way there. Doesn't appear there has been a first plowing on that side of the road."

"Don't know. Probably plowing Cheryl Road first. He tends to start with his own street first," Pat said. The windshield wipers brushed over the glass, streaking frozen water. Lumps of melting snow streaked down from the top of the frame, brushed away as the wipers swept again. "God, I hate January. I hate *winter*."

"I hate Stoll," Weller muttered. Pat felt a bit of nervous tension. He checked the radio transmitter to ensure it wasn't accidentally pressed. He'd hate to have Weller's tirade about the Sheriff broadcast over the department's frequency.

"Trust me, I'd rather be in the office sipping coffee too," Pat said.

"Guy hates my guts, that's why he sent *us* to patrol out here in the middle of nowhere…during a winter storm. Doing roadside assistance."

"Well, he at least has a point," Pat said. "Cell reception is almost non-existent out here, especially in weather like this. If anyone got in an accident or stranded, they'd be screwed."

"Yeah…that was US," Weller said.

"True," Pat said.

"Now our shovel is busted, so now I really hope we don't have to dig anyone out."

"You know what you should've done," Pat said, "is you should've siphoned out some gas, poured it onto the snow and lit it. Would've melted it right away."

"Yeah, smart," Weller said. "Take the gas out from the car…during a snowstorm, twenty miles from town. And you wonder why I don't let you do my taxes."

"Ouch."

"Besides, I'd be surprised if I could even get my lighter to spark in this cold."

Pat suddenly got excited.

"That's the good part actually," he said. "You don't use a lighter, you use a taser! I saw a video of an arrest. The perp's shirt was covered in lighter fluid from a cookout or something, and he tried to run. The cop got him with the taser, and *whoosh*, the shirt went right up and—" A loud *thump* echoed from under the bumper and the Interceptor pitched upward. "Oh shit!" The rear of the vehicle bumped up as the rear tires passed over the huge lump. Pat pulled the steering wheel to the left as the Interceptor began to fishtail.

Weller braced a hand on the dashboard and another against the door as he tensed. The Interceptor completed a full spin before they watched their view of the road angle off. The vehicle dipped over the edge of the road, its spin halted suddenly by a heavy smashing sound along the bumper near the rear passenger tire. Pat caught his breath and looked back over his shoulder. He could see the tree branch pressing against the cracked rear windshield. He eased on the accelerator. The tires spun freely beneath him, with no traction.

"Nice going, gas man. I oughta tase *you*," Weller said.

"Hey, it wasn't me!" Pat said defensively. The wind swung their doors open as they stepped out of the car. They walked to the rear of the vehicle. The bumper was caved in near the axle by the tree trunk. Pat looked past the tree, realizing it was a blessing in disguise. Had they not hit it, they would've ended up rolling down a hill, likely would've flipped over.

"Now Sheriff will really have our asses," Weller said.

"Oh, relax," Pat said. He watched as the Corporal reached under the wheel. The tire was deflating, though it didn't appear to have any branches sticking out of it. Snow was bunched in thick mounds under the axles. Considering the slope the vehicle was positioned in, they'd be hard pressed to dig themselves out this time.

"Not relaxing," Weller said. "Is the engine alright?" Pat went around to the front.

"Yeah, it's fine. Not that it'll do us any good. We're stuck," he said.

"Yeah, I gathered that part. You wanna spray some gas and shoot your taser? Maybe that'll get us unstuck," Weller said.

"Hey, I was driving straight," Pat said. Weller joined him at the front bumper. He knelt down, noticing scrapes under the bumper.

"That wasn't a snowbank," he said. "What the hell did you hit?"

Pat shrugged his shoulders. Both deputies walked up the hill, grimacing as the wind blew in their faces. They followed their tire tracks, which formed a spiraling loop for several meters before it straightened into a level path.

"There!" Pat pointed. He withdrew his hand as several flakes of snow hit his face. He gripped the collar of his jacket and lifted it to his mouth, covering everything but his eyes. "We hit around here. I don't see any…" his boot hit something hard. Pat knelt down to feel it. "What the hell is this?"

The wind whistled in his ears as Weller bent down to feel the object. Whatever it was, it was solid and heavy. It had an edge. A jagged edge. Weller pulled his hand away as he realized he was feeling the tip of a metal splinter.

"You know what it is?" Pat asked.

"It's a part of a frame," Weller said.

"Like, for a trailer?"

"I think so." The two deputies moved along the edge of the object, brushing the snow off of it. Red metal emerged, with ice accumulated along it. Weller was right: it was the frame of a cox trailer. It was bent into a disproportionate shape, some of the metal sticking outward.

"What is this doing out here across the road…" Pat stopped, suddenly deep in thought. Staring at the snow around him, he realized the logic of what probably happened. He turned his gaze to the edge of the road. "Oh, shit." The brush along the side of the road had been ripped out by the roots and completely flattened. Lower branches had been ripped from the surrounding trees as though a train had plowed between them. There were no tire marks, but even if there were, they would've likely been covered up by the snow. The debris was barely visible, as most of it was buried. Even the larger branches that stuck through the snow were heavily obscured, not just by the compacted snow, but the white dust that blew in the air over it.

Snow crunched under their boots as the two deputies approached the ruins. Behind the trees was a small hill, leading down a similar path they narrowly avoided themselves. The air was dark, the grey sunlight obscured further by the trees. In that darkness were two beams of light that streamed deep into the belly of the forest. Weller pulled a flashlight from his duty belt and shone it into the forest. The light bounced back in red gleams as it reflected the tail lights of a black Dodge pickup truck. It was wedged between the trunks of two maple trees, the passenger door crumpled inward. Bare branches stretched over the hood like demonic hands.

"Oh, Jesus," Pat muttered. They hurried down the hill as fast as they could, making sure to plant each step carefully to keep from toppling over.

As they entered the woods, the wind sustained itself into a deep drone. Snow fell in large clumps as they weighed down the fir branches around them. With much of the snow congested within the trees, the tire treads were partially visible beneath the thin layers of white. The ground and brush had been pushed into tiny mounds along the path.

The engine was still running. In fact, the vehicle was still trying to coast. Weller stepped along the driver's side and shined his light into the window. There was nothing in the seat but windshield glass and a couple of snack items. Above it, snow was whipping around in circles as though caught in a funnel. The heat was still blasting away, the music still playing. What was most bizarre was that the lever was still set to *drive*.

Weller walked around the front of the vehicle and shone his light through the windshield. The whole left-hand side was busted inward, the shards all over the dashboard and seat. The right half was thoroughly cracked near to the point of shattering.

"Must've hit a branch on his way down," Pat said.

"Then where is it?" Weller said. Weller panned his flashlight all around. "Better question is, where is *he*?" He looked deep into the woods, seeing nothing but snow and trees. A few stray streaks of light streamed in from the sunset. Otherwise, it was dark. As he turned back to examine the truck, the light passed over the hood of the truck. It was crumbled down in at least four places. He found it odd that there weren't any other scratches aside from the dent areas themselves. It almost appeared like someone slammed a hammer to the thing. He stared at it, then felt his fingers around the indentations.

*Ramming into the woods would do that to an engine*, he thought. Then again, he couldn't help but notice that there didn't seem to be any sticks or branches around the engine itself. Nor were there any inside the vehicle. Not even a pine cone from what he could see. Even if the branch had been shaken loose, it would leave some sort of residue.

"How long you think it's been there?" Pat asked. Weller turned around and looked up through the trail at the road.

"We didn't see any tread. Storm started hitting hard about three hours ago. Assuming he hit a patch of ice, I would assume the crash happened around then. But..." he stopped and panned the light back into the woods, "where the hell did he go?"

"If he went off on foot, there'd be footprints in the snow," Pat said. "I doubt he would've wandered in deeper. He probably got picked up by somebody before the storm got bad. Probably felt no sense in notifying the police."

"And they just left the engine running? Didn't even switch it into *park*?"

Pat stood quiet, realizing the good and obvious point.

"Want me to call it in?" he asked.

"In a minute. Let's get the plate and take a look inside to see if we find anything to identify the driver." The interior light illuminated as Weller opened the door. The seat cushion was wet from the snow that had spilled in and melted from the heater. Huge shards of glass were all over the place, forcing Weller to be extra careful. He snapped a picture with his phone before checking the passenger seat. As he started moving around, something in the back seat caught his eye. It was a tool bag and jackhammer.

"Guy was probably a construction worker," Weller said. He examined the glass on the seat. Some of them had small tints of blood on them, dried up in the heat. When it caved in, it caved in on the driver. But it wasn't much blood. He looked at what remained of the windshield, specifically the jagged shards that stuck from the lower frame. The interior lights shined over the frozen blood had crusted along the edges. Pat moved beside him and took a look.

"You think he tossed through the windshield?"

"The glass was busted in, not out. But then again, it doesn't look like the seatbelt is clipped…" Weller paused and looked again at the seat. The seatbelt buckle wasn't there. He checked to see if it had gotten tucked between the cushion and the center console, but it wasn't even there. "The hell?"

"Uh, Ron, look at this," Pat said, pointing to the hanging seatbelt. Weller backed from the seat and examined the belt. The tongue was resting at the foot of the seat, still attached to the buckle. The end of the nylon strap was frizzled, having been torn right out from its place.

Pat opened the center console and dug inside for the registration, ignoring the distracting howl of the wind. Snow fell in huge clumps from the branches, crackling the brush below as he pulled out the vehicle registration.

"Brett Silverman," he read it aloud. "Proof of insurance says the same." He noticed the light reflecting off something on the footpad. He switched on his flashlight and shined it down. It was an iPhone 6s. It was held inside a plastic belt clip, which had snapped into pieces. Pat snapped a picture before picking up the item. He attempted to turn it on in the hope of getting a list of contacts. The phone was locked. It wouldn't have mattered much, as the battery was nearly drained.

"Hang on to that. If this person isn't found, one of the tech guys will wanna unlock it," Weller said.

Pat tucked the iPhone into his coat pocket. After slamming the door shut he started walking back up the hill. He glanced back, seeing Weller wandering in front of the truck. He was turning over fallen branches and studying the terrain. "Find something?"

"I don't know," Weller said. The brush had been bent outward, almost appearing as though something with large mass had scraped its way through this area. Moose perhaps, then again, moose didn't usually leave a trail like that. Perhaps it was his mind messing with him. The drone of the wind was not helping, nor was the intense cold.

"What is it, then?" Pat called out. He had to raise his voice to be heard over the wind. He was both curious and impatient.

"Get back up to the car and radio Dispatch and get them to send some more units out here. I'm gonna keep looking. If there's any more evidence, we don't want it buried by the snow," Weller said.

"You want me to give you a hand?"

"No, I'd rather you stay up there in case someone happens to drive by."

Deputy Pat could barely hear him over the wind but was able to catch enough to get the gist. "Okay. Don't stray too far." He climbed up the small hill, stomping his feet over huge lumps of snow.

Weller gazed back at the engine hood, his eyes fixed on those strange indentations. In each one was a similar abrasion to the paint. Two large creases, spaced perfectly apart, had marked each dent.

*Odd that they have the same exact mark.* If any individual one had that mark, he would think nothing of it. But all three? Each with the exact same mark? Weller wasn't sure what to make of it. Then again...

He looked at the flattened bushes again.

...He wasn't sure what to make of any of this.

# CHAPTER 2

Pat sat in the driver's seat and blasted the heat in his face. Rubbing his hands together, he watched the snow raining down onto the car. The overhead flashers cast a red and blue glow over the huge mounds. It would soon be the only light they'd have. The hood was almost completely buried and the windshield wipers were struggling to keep up with the accumulation, despite the heater blasting away. Several trees rocked back and forth. Deep in the forest, he could hear the echoes of cracking branches succumbing to the weight of snow and ice.

Pat was growing antsy. He looked back over the horizon. The sun would be set in about an hour. He hoped someone would be by before then. The last thing he wanted was to be stuck all the way out here at night in this kind of weather.

He checked his watch. Weller was still down there observing the scene. Been doing so for the last thirty minutes. If he found the driver, he would've likely radioed it in.

He clicked the transmitter on his radio.

"How's it going out there, sport?" He released the transmitter and waited for a response. "Corporal? What's going on?"

"*Has anyone shown up yet?*"

"Oh, jeez! Dude you scared me," Pat said, his voice raised. "And, no." "Alrig—Keep me—" Weller's voice was lost in the howl of the wind. The storm was filling his microphone, making it nearly impossible for Pat to understand what he was saying.

"Say again," Pat said. "Ron? Shit." He clipped the mic back to his shirt and leaned back. Watching the snow swirling along the road like tiny white tornadoes, he hated the idea of letting Weller walk the woods alone. With the radio being unreliable, if anything were to happen, and it could happen with all the branches coming down in the storm, he would never know. And who knew how far Weller was venturing.

"Damn it," he muttered. He opened the door, which nearly flew from his hand as the wind took hold of it. He slammed the door shut and briefly observed the Interceptor. The wind gusts had rolled piles of snow against the wheels. If it wasn't impossible to get out before, it was now. He pulled his winter hat down as far as he could. Fighting against the wind, he trekked down toward the opening in the brush.

********

Balls of white rained from the trees, trailing a mist that glistened in the beam of Weller's flashlight. The truck was probably a hundred meters behind him, the headlights now appearing like two yellow balls from where he stood.

Weller walked along the battered trail where he had seen the crushed bushes near the truck. The path, however brief it was, seemed to curve left toward Devil's Rock before disappearing. Of course, that was with the assumption that it was even a path. It was the woods, after all, in a winter storm. But it was weird: that bush was pressed down, as though something with significant weight had passed over it. Wind wouldn't do that, and the truck had stopped short of it.

One thing was for sure, the driver of the truck was nowhere to be seen. With no confirmation that he was dead or picked up, it was imperative that he be found. Or else, he would freeze to death in this weather.

Weller slowly walked out, panning his light to-and-fro. For a while, all he could see were the swaying branches of pine trees, dripping debris along with patches of snow. The woods grew darker as he ventured in deeper.

"Hello!" he called out. His voice was muffled by the wind. "Anyone out there?!" There was no response. He started to consider it was best to go back and wait in the car. He started to turn, his light brushing over the trunk of a huge maple tree. In the corner of his eye, he noticed the strange gash in the bark.

With the light fixed on it, he approached. It was an oddly shaped mark, almost appearing like a cat claw, only with two tails instead of four. The two creases were almost V-shaped. Weller kneeled down at the base of the tree, brushing away snow to gently reveal the ground below. There they were, scraps of bark freshly severed from place.

There was something else there too. Weller dug a little harder, keeping his light fixed on the spot. The snow had clumped pretty firmly, making it difficult to brush away. But he could see the edge of something sticking out from under it. It was soft and flexible, not part of the tree. Hammering down with his fist, he broke apart the snow and brushed it aside. His light beamed down on a glove. It was grey in color and made of wool.

Weller noticed something: a discoloration near the cuff. He secured his light to a pouch on his jacket before picking up the glove. With the beam fixed on it, he pulled the cuff apart. Dried blood crusted the inside, along with a few tiny strands of hair. Shining the light close to the exterior, he could see tiny bits of bark entrenched in the fabric.

"What the hell?"

"Christ!" Weller jumped up and spun, dropping the glove as he staggered back from Pat's flashlight. Pat held a hand up, his eyes wide as he saw Weller's hand instinctively go for his Glock. A moment later, the hand moved away. Weller sucked in a deep breath and released a long sharp exhale.

"I thought you were gonna wait in the car."

"Do I look like a five-year old?" Pat said.

"You do have the baby-face thing going on," Weller said. He was still catching his breath. The attempt at humor did little to lessen the anxiety he felt.

"What's the word on backup?"

"Nobody's here yet. I don't know how long it'll take," Pat said. He shined his light on the dropped glove. "Was that blood I saw?"

"Yes," Weller said. He turned and pointed ahead of them. "He must've gone that way. I don't understand why. Wouldn't it make more sense to go to the road?"

"Even if he was bleeding, I'm surprised he'd take it off. His hand must be frozen by now," Pat remarked.

"Maybe he was dazed in the crash. Doesn't know where he's going?"

"That would explain why he left his cell phone behind," Pat mentioned. Weller paused, remembering that detail. It was strange that he didn't call 9-1-1, even if he was injured. Then again, all they were doing at this point was speculating. Hell, they weren't even sure the glove was the driver's. Only one thing was certain. Whatever occurred, it wasn't a normal traffic incident.

*"Car Six calling Car Two. I'm on site."*

"Oh, figures they'd show up when I'm not up there," Pat said. He grabbed the mic from under his jacket and lifted it to his mouth. "Ten-Four, Six. Wait there, we'll be coming out."

*"Copy."*

Pat tucked the mic away and started walking back. He glanced over at Weller, who was still busy inspecting the ground.

"You're the ranking officer. You coming?"

Weller seemed to ignore him while continuing to look the area over with his flashlight. He had walked over to the next tree and was studying a solidified substance that had accumulated on its trunk. It almost resembled dried sap, though he didn't think that was what it was. It almost had a stringy texture to it. He touched it with his glove. It was rigid like dried honey that had dripped down the tree onto the ground in several streams.

"Corporal?" Pat said. Weller glanced back at him. He could see the red and blue glints streaking from the road as Car Six pulled up near the crash scene. Pat was right, it was his responsibility to take charge until the Sheriff arrived.

The two of them hiked back to the crash. The twirling flashers grew brighter as they came close to the tree line. They could see a figure standing at the opening in the brush where the truck came down. He held a flashlight in one hand and a cup of coffee in the other.

Deputy McCarter lifted the cup as though having a toast to Weller and Pat's arrival.

"You guys are lucky you didn't have a nice little tumble down there yourselves," he said, pointing his elbow at their Interceptor.

"It hasn't been the best of days," Weller said. He stepped up the hill and tucked his chin into his jacket collar. The wind was more intense out in the open. Snowflakes struck his face like icy mosquitos. "Is it just you?"

"Yeah, for now."

"Sheriff not coming?" Weller asked.

"He's on his way. It'll take them a while to get out here. A lot of the guys are tied up with traffic reports down town," McCarter said. The thirty-five-year-old tilted the cup into his mouth and swallowed a large gulp. "I happened to be nearby; Sheriff had me on roadside patrol like you. Took me forever to get here, though. These roads, man."

"I know. They're bad. And where the hell is Matt?"

"You haven't seen him either?" McCarter said.

"No."

"Weird."

"What about the State? Any word from them?" Pat asked.

"Dispatch is working on getting ahold of them," McCarter answered. "Like us, they're wrapped up with traffic accidents all over the interstate."

"Well, unless any of them involve a missing person..." Pat remarked.

"That's the point we're making to them," McCarter said. "Truth is, who knows how long it'll be to get anyone out here. For all we know, the Highway Patrol will get here before Stoll."

Both deputies looked at Weller.

"So, what do you want us to do? Wait?" Pat asked.

"It's an option," McCarter added. "This storm should let up in a couple of hours. It'll be on-and-off wind gusts after that."

Weller stared down into the woods, then at the darkening grey in the horizon. The light would soon be gone, making the search much more difficult. Storm or no storm, the longer they waited, the greater the probability they would be searching for a body.

"McCarter, you wait here in case the guy comes back. His name is probably Brett Silverman. At least, that's who the truck is registered to."

"You're going back in?" McCarter asked.

"Don't have much choice," Weller said. "We're the only ones here. We know the guy was alive long enough to take off his glove..." *Or was it scraped off?* Weller remembered the residue of bark in the wool. The more he thought of the whole situation, the weirder it seemed.

"That's gonna be a tough haul," McCarter said. "There's no trail near this neck of the woods. The nearest road is a mile back that way."

"That's what we're gonna hike toward," Weller said. "As long as we keep going that way, we'll reach...which is it... Boyer Road?"

"That's right. Can't miss it."

"If another unit show up during that time, direct them that way, will ya?"

"Will do," McCarter said.

"Great," Pat muttered.

"You're coming. Don't complain," Weller said.

"Me? Complain?" Pat glanced at McCarter. "You don't happen to have any more of that coffee, do ya?" The Deputy shook his head. "Yeah, that's what I figured."

"Come on, Charlie," Weller said. With a heavy sigh, Pat followed the Corporal into the woods. Flashlights beamed from their uniforms, waving back and forth as they ventured inward.

# CHAPTER 3

Their boots disappeared into an ocean of white that covered the forest floor. Taking a single step was becoming a challenge, as they had to literally raise their knees high to plant their feet ahead of them. The one good thing about the exercise was that it was keeping them warm. That was all Pat could focus on. He hated the deep view of the woods. The lights shined on either thick pines, empty maples, or empty background. But even the space between the trees wasn't empty. Leaves and snow swirled in wild displays, stirring up sheets of white mist.

"Hello?" Corporal Weller called out again. "This is the Sheriff's Department! Is there anyone out there?" As usual, there was no answer. Even if anyone was out there, it'd be a miracle if they heard him. Weller's voice was barely able to get over the wind.

And Pat hated that wind. Not only the howl, but the constant waving of branches overhead. They made sure to keep away from the maple trees, which were more likely to rain debris. Then again, it wasn't too smart to stick close to the pines. The wind was shaking their pine needles loose, mixing them in with the snow beneath.

Pat glanced back to see if he could see the truck lights or the flashers. There was nothing but grey air and the swaying bodies of trees. And so far, no evidence of anyone having been through here.

"How far is the road?" Pat asked.

"I'm not sure," Weller said. Pat jumped as a branch cracked in the distance. He turned his flashlight toward the sound just in time to see an eight-foot long arm of a tree angle downward, the tip smashing against the earth.

Weller was beginning to share his buddy's apprehensiveness. He was now looking up, shining the yellow light into the canopy to make sure nothing was about to come down directly above them.

"Let's just keep moving northwest and we'll be out of this," Weller said.

"Fine by me," Pat said. He turned to face Weller. "Ron, I'm not trying to be the one to call the shots, but I don't think this guy's alive. And if he is, I don't think he's in these woods."

"Where else could he be?"

"If he's alive…and didn't get picked up, then he probably hiked to Boyer Road. That leads down to the lake. There are some cabins down that way. If he's still alive, maybe he's taking refuge in one of them."

Weller considered the possibility. It certainly wasn't out of the realm.

"Seems odd that he would walk through the woods to do it, and not along the road…" his voice trailed off. Pat noticed him looking past him, then turned to see whatever it was he was looking at.

"What is it?"

"I don't know," Weller said. He started walking to the north. Pat followed him, carefully watching each step.

Weller weaved between a few fir trees then slowed his walk. His light was fixed on a strange lump in the snow. Pat saw it and swallowed hard.

"Did we find…?"

"No. Not a body," Weller said. But it was something, and it had a bit of bulk to it. He slowly approached the lump and carefully brushed the snow off of it. The material easily bent inward as he touched it. Whatever it was, it was hollow. The snow fell off, revealing a tan color.

"A Carhart?" Pat said. Weller didn't say anything as he lifted the heavy coat. A lot of dirt had been frozen onto the material. The jacket itself was stiff, having been left in the cold for a significant period of time. He checked the pockets for any identification but found nothing. Pat swung his light all around, looking for any other items. "You think it belonged to the missing person?"

"I can't say," Weller said. He tried to open the coat. Even after being meddled with, it was still very stiff. "I don't think so. I think it's been out here for a hell of a while." He looked up, his eyes widening with increased interest. He placed the coat down and stepped over it.

Just a few yards away, a huge pine branch had been snapped from its base. The arm, still attached to the tree by a few strands, leaned down to the ground, its many needle-filled extensions forming a wall between them and the tree.

"It's a tree," Pat remarked. "Branches fall. It's been happening all over, in case you haven't noticed." Weller stared at it for a few more moments. The needles had all turned brown. The wood was dead. The rest of the tree was alive and flourishing. This had to have broken down at least a month ago. And judging by the way the arm was bent inward, it seemed as though it was weighed down by something.

But it was something on the stem of the branch itself that interested him. There were a couple of scrapes on it, which perfectly resembled the mark he had seen on the other tree near the crash site. This mark was darker and not nearly as fresh as the other one.

"Hey, Ron! Come look at this!"

Pat's voice shook Weller into reality. He looked to his right, seeing Pat's light swaying back and forth as he stepped over branches and bushes. Whatever he saw, it was enough to make him move quick.

Weller hustled to catch up with him, squinting as the cold air stung his eyes. Twigs snapped and snow crunched under his muck boots as he caught up. Winding around a tree, he realized what Pat had found.

His eyes watched as the tarp of a tent flapped in the wind. The base of the small shelter was crushed inward. The stakes were deep in the ground, the opening lifting with each gust of the wind like the mouth of a hungry beast. In front of it were numerous camping items, including an open bag of charcoal laying near some unused firewood. In the center of the camp was an empty firepit.

Weller stepped toward the camp. With one hand gripping his Glock, he slowly lifted the opening. He took a breath, apprehensive to what he might see inside.

The interior was empty, save for a sleeping bag and a few scattered items. Books were scattered along with a pair of shoes and reading glasses. There were a couple of blankets, all appearing clean except for the dirt that had gotten inside the tent. He stood up all the way, widening the tent as best as he could. In the back was a hiking bag and a two-foot long tube, designed for carrying disassembled fishing poles.

And the fishing poles were present, laying just a couple of feet from the firepit. They were geared with fish hooks and weights, as though waiting to be taken to the lake. He was certain of one thing: this was no hobo setup. It simply appeared to be a genuine private vacation.

"What the hell happened?" Pat said.

"This is no winter setup," Weller said. He glanced all around. "Where the hell is the camper?"

"Nobody just goes out and abandons this stuff," Pat said. Weller started digging inside the tent once more, ruffling the books and clothes. A set of house keys rattled as they fell from the pile. Weller sorted through the pants' pockets, finally locating a wallet.

"Dispatch?" he waited. No response came through. "Dispatch, come in."

"*Hey, Corporal. It's McCarter. I don't think they're catching your transmission.*"

"It's the damn storm. He's the only one close enough to hear us," Pat muttered.

"Shh. Hey, McCarter. Give Dispatch a TX. We found what looks to be an abandoned campsite."

"*Campsite? Somebody living out there?*"

"No, it just looks like a typical hiker camp," Weller said. "Looks like it's been here a while. Have Dispatch run a name." He opened the wallet and pulled out the driver's license. "Jeffery Stepp. S-T-E-P-P. Date of birth: March 21$^{st}$, 1985."

"*Copy that. Give me a minute.*"

Weller flipped through the wallet's contents. It contained three twenty-dollar bills, a credit card, debit card, and a couple of miscellaneous photos. Nothing to indicate a homeless person. As he speculated, it appeared to be the belongings of a regular hiker.

Pat continued digging through the camp, examining all the scattered items. The charcoal bag was almost full. There was a small bottle of lighter fluid laying near the pit. A few split logs lay scattered, with a few larger logs pulled up to be used as seats. This person had been here long enough to make himself at home. Pat walked to one of the logs to take a seat.

The toe of his boot hit something solid near the edge of the log. Pat froze for a moment and looked down, unable to see whatever it was due to the snow. He knelt down and gently brushed away the snow. Clumps of snow rolled into small mounds as he unburied the object.

The glint of metal reflected his flashlight. Pat realized he was looking at a slug-nose Taurus revolver, covered by a thin dusting of snow.

"Ron?"

"Yeah?"

"We have a firearm down here."

"You're shitting me."

"You know me," Pat said. He took a photo before picking it up. He opened the cylinder and removed the cartridges. "All six of them have been fired."

"Jot down the serial number and let's get back to the road," Weller said. "We've probably got a body somewhere out here."

"Already done," Pat said. He snapped a close-up shot of the serial number then placed the firearm down. "Jesus, man. How is it that nobody's reported this camp till now?"

"Nowhere near the trail. It's a half mile from the road, blocked by thick forest. Got nothing but pines near the road. Can't even see five feet into the woods. My guess, this fella was looking for a private spot."

*"Corporal Weller, this is McCarter!"*

Weller was surprised by the urgency in his voice. He grabbed his mic and hunched low to protect it from the wind.

"Go ahead, Car-Six."

*"That didn't take long, Boss. When that name and date of birth was entered into the computers, it set off all kinds of red flags."*

"Elaborate, please," Weller said.

*"Jeffrey Stepp was last seen sometime in late October. Family reports said he enjoyed camping and hiking in the late season, and usually took busses and tried different locations. He was reported missing on November 7th."*

Weller stood silent, his jaw slack as his mind absorbed the information. He locked eyes with Pat, who shared the same dreaded look. Near his foot was the revolver, the cylinder open, the cartridges empty. Weller's gaze moved beyond the camp, to the base of a nearby pine. Twelve feet beside it was a baby maple tree. Its life was cut short, its height never to expand beyond five feet, as its trunk had been snapped near the roots.

The wind kicked up, causing the tent to sway in rhythm with the trees. The tarp rolled back until the stakes prevented it from going any further, revealing the handle to another fishing pole. At the end of the line were the rotted remains of a trout, now frozen in stasis from the cold. In its mouth was a hook, still embedded in its lip.

# CHAPTER 4

Pat tugged up on the collar of his coat, pressing the lining of fur into his skin. He felt his teeth starting to chatter uncontrollably. Weller was still walking the perimeter, digging through branches and bushes for any sign of the camper.

The light was fading. By now, they were almost completely reliant on their flashlights. Pat walked another circle, more to maintain warmth than to locate a body. He flinched as he watched a huge shower of snow rain down the side of a thirty-foot pine. The whole side of the tree writhed as the branches bent down, giving in to the weight of the condensed snow. He whipped around to the sound of another crackling branch in the distance. Wherever it was, it was obscured by the dark. Not that he would see it anyway. The wind played havoc on his eyes, and the snow gusted in sheets between the trees.

Weller took one last look at the camp, then gazed up at the surrounding forest.

"What's taking everyone so long?" he mumbled to himself. He already knew the answer, but the conditions were making him impatient. The realization came that there was nothing more to be done at this time. If there was a body out here, they'd never find it in these conditions.

"If you want, we can expand our search this way," Pat said. He pointed southward. Weller considered it, then shook his head.

"No. Let's get on out of here," he said. "It's getting late. And…we've been out here long enough."

"We'll probably be right back anyways when the Highway Patrol gets here," Pat muttered. "If they ever show." In the meantime, it was the answer Pat was hoping to hear from Weller. He aimed his flashlight all over the place, trying to regain his sense of direction. "Which way is the road?"

"This way," Weller said.

"Thank God one of us is paying attention," Pat quipped. The two deputies started marching through snow and brush on their way to Boyer Road. Both of them looked ahead, hoping they could see the sparkle of flashers.

However, the only light to be seen was the shine of their own flashlights. The sun had completed its dip in the horizon, leaving them in perpetual darkness. Their pace slowed, as it became harder not to trip over the natural debris along the forest floor.

Pat grabbed his radio mic extender and squeezed the transmitter.

"Car Six. McCarter? You there?" The radio traffic was silent. Pat grimaced in frustration. *I knew it!* He tried again. "McCarter. Come in, will ya?" As he dreadfully expected, the signal was not getting through in the storm. He cursed himself mentally for not suggesting that McCarter go ahead and meet them at Boyer Road. "Just my night."

"Don't worry. We're almost to the road," Weller said.

"Yeah? And how are we gonna get back? You honestly expect me to walk a half-mile up Boyer Road, then a mile back to our car?"

"You have a better plan?"

"I thought I did, but as you saw, it didn't pan out," Pat said.

"Someone will pick us up. They should be arriving by now. Lord knows they've had plenty of time, even in this weather."

"We've probably traveled more on foot then they have on wheels," Pat muttered. He kept pace with Weller as they stomped over huge piles of snow. He could feel some of the snow melting through the lace holes in his boots. The wet sensation in his socks grew very annoying, very quickly. He was starting to envy Weller's muck boots.

*Perks of being a horse-owner, I guess.*

Pat kept his eyes on the stream that projected from his flashlight as he panned it over the terrain. The last thing he wanted to do was to unwittingly stumble on the frozen corpse of either of their missing persons. And he was certain there was a corpse. Somewhere.

The thought was making him jumpy. Now every shadow appeared to have an ominous posture, as though taunting him with each step. Each one added to the worry of a potential crazed maniac hiding somewhere in these woods.

"Up this way," Weller yelled over the wind. Pat's eyes followed the Corporal's light. It streamed past a thick barrier of trees into empty space. Pat released a sigh of relief. That empty space was the road.

The reprieve of stepping out of the woods was brief, as the wind intensified the instant he stepped out of the tree line. Snow ripped through the air, pummeling the trees on the other side. There were street lights lining the road, though they were few and far between. Some of them flickered, their power lines struggling to stay attached. The sky was dark and starless. The snow had amassed in a thick white body that stretched the length of the road. Weller stepped inward, his foot disappearing up to two inches above his heel.

There was no sign of any patrol vehicles.

Pat's hand slapped down on his sides.

"Not looking forward to the sinus infection I'll get from this," he said. "We should've gone back the way we came."

"You know very well we'd have gotten turned around," Weller said. He looked around. He was certain backup would have arrived by now. He bared his teeth as the cold wind assaulted him.

"Hey, down that way!" Pat pointed to the right. Weller gazed into the distance. Down the curvy path of the road was the shine of headlights.

"Oh, good," Weller said.

"You think it's a squad car?"

"I'm not sure. Whoever it is, I think they're parked. The lights don't seem to be moving." He grabbed his mic and spoke into it, "Corporal Weller calling for any unit. Anyone out on Boyer road?"

"*I--…Be advised--… miles--…*"

"Please repeat." Weller heard nothing but static as the wind and terrain messed with the signal. "Son of a bitch." Warm breath blew from his mouth with each word. He glanced over his shoulder toward the main road, hoping to see that red-and-blue shine. There was nothing but night air and snow.

"Wanna go down there?" Pat asked.

"It's the opposite way of where we need to go," Weller said. "If it's not a cop, then that's more distance we'll have to trek to get back."

"Hell, I have no shame. I'll just ask this fella for a ride," Pat said.

"And if he's stuck as well?"

"I'll dig him out with my bare hands at this point. Besides, what if he's seen our missing driver?"

Weller nodded. It was a good point. Pat didn't wait to listen for a response. He stomped through the snow, almost resembling the famous image of Bigfoot as he marched along the side of the road. Weller hustled to catch up with him. As they went, the flickering streetlight went black.

# CHAPTER 5

It was a quarter mile walk down to the vehicle. As the road curved slightly to the right, they were able to get a better view.

Pat slowed down and squinted. The headlights were vertical. He could see the tires facing out toward the road. The truck had been turned over. They quickened their pace, eventually closing the distance.

The truck was laying on its passenger side, the engine facing their direction. A red plow stuck out from the snow, having detached during the crash. Weller pointed his flashlight into the shattered windshield. The interior was empty. The keys were in the ignition and the lever was set to *drive*, although the engine was not running this time. The hood was battered, the grill dented far inward as though it hit something solid.

"Is this Matt Williams' truck?" Pat called to Weller. The Corporal nodded. He felt the hood of the engine. It was cold, though not ice cold. Looking behind the truck, he could see the faint signs of tread, and the mounds along the road from Matt's initial plow before it ended here. Behind the truck, the snow had been whipped around in a frenzy, likely from the tires during a spinout.

"He's not here," Weller said. He flashed his light back at the road. There didn't appear to be any debris or obstacles. "I don't get it. What the hell did he hit? He's not the type to drive like a crazed—" As his light came back over the hood of the truck, he noticed the same scratch marks. Pat moved up beside him and stared at the creases.

"What the hell is that?" Pat said.

"I don't know," Weller said. "They were on the Dodge, and one of the trees back near the other crash." Pat knelt down to get a better look through the busted windshield.

"There's blood on the steering wheel," he said. "If he's still alive, he's hurt bad."

"This didn't happen too long ago," Weller said. "It definitely took place after the other crash."

"If he's on foot, he probably went to the lake. It's only a half mile down that way," Pat said.

"Maybe," Weller said. "All I know is that we need to find him. There are no other tire tracks, meaning nobody else has driven through here. We need to coordinate with the other car units and—"

His eyes caught sight of an indentation in the snow. He swept his light out, spotting another a few feet away, then another. There were several, each spaced out by a few feet.

"Footprints?" Pat asked.

"I don't know. They look like tracks, though he'd have to take damn long strides. Matt's a pretty tall guy, but still." The tracks were widely spaced, each about the size of a human footprint, though they were more circular in shape. The snow had filled them in, though not entirely, which could account for the odd shape. That being if they were even footprints.

Pat followed the path, noticing a separate set of tracks about twelve feet to the left. They were of the same shape, not quite evenly spaced out.

*Perhaps he had somebody with him?*

Both sets of tracks disappeared into the trees on the opposite side of the road.

"I hate that I'm suggesting this, but we should probably check if he's in there."

Weller examined the direction of the tracks.

"It's possible he went in there to get out of the wind," he said. He sighed. He wasn't eager to wander through any more forest. He had nearly tripped at least five times between here and the camp. But Pat was right. They had an obligation to check. If Matt was lost in these woods, it would only be a matter of time before he'd succumb to the cold. "Alright, just a quick gander. I don't want to miss our ride."

They followed the tracks across the road and through the space between the trees. Both trails narrowed together, almost forming an arrow as they converged into the gap of a pine and maple tree. Twigs snapped under their boots as they entered the forest. The debris was only a couple of inches under the snow, sandwiched against another few inches that accumulated under it.

Their flashlights illuminated a series of twisting shapes. Snow rained down to the forest floor, knocking loose pine needles and cones. But even the snow on the ground was only partially visible, as it was covered by numerous branches that had broken free.

"Mr. Williams!" Pat called out.

"Matt!"

Both deputies staggered in surprise as another branch cracked in the distance. Immediately, they both had decided they'd only venture in a little bit more. Every moment spent in these woods was a hazard. Even a clump of snow, if given enough height, could cause serious injury.

"Let's check over here," Pat said, pointing to another trail of prints. They were barely visible, obscured by the plant life and wind. The trail led them to the trunk of a rotting tree. With no way to go around it, Pat swung himself over, his feet crunching old twigs as he landed on the other side. Weller followed right behind him.

His hand touched down on the trunk as he lifted himself over. He set down on the other side and straightened his posture to continue, only to feel the sudden jolt from being stuck. His hand would not come off the log.

"The hell?"

He grabbed his left arm by the wrist and pulled upward. His hand lifted slowly from the log, trailing a thick, stringy substance along with it. A loud grunt left his lungs as he struggled.

Pat turned and watched, his light reflecting off the thick substance that clung to Weller's glove. He approached for a better view. Whatever it was, it appeared to be in the process of solidifying. It was brownish in color, with a sap-like texture. The strands thinned and stretched as Weller pulled away from it. With enough leverage, he turned his wrist and looked at the palm of his glove. The substance clung on tight. Tiny strands had messed together, making it impossible for him to move his fingers. Even if he broke away, there'd be no getting the residual sap off his glove.

"Screw it," he said, removing the glove entirely.

"That's not tree sap, is it?" Pat asked.

"I don't think so. Whatever it is, it's all over this log and…all over the trail." Weller noticed hints of this brown goo glistening in a hardened state along the branches. It hung in tiny webs along the bushes, stringing to the trunk of a nearby tree. They followed the substance to the tree and stared at the stringy entanglements along the bark. It had a wet appearance, despite being hardened. They could see the individual droplets that formed the streams before it solidified.

Below the substance were two sets of tracks. Each footprint was spaced out by a few feet, with at least ten feet space between the trails. Between them was a steady indentation in the snow that followed in the same path, as though a huge snake had slithered through here.

Or something had been dragged.

Golden streams of light found nothing but forest as the two deputies followed the trail. Shadows danced in odd angles with each movement of the flashlights. The trail went deep into the forest into higher terrain as it approached Devil's Rock.

"How far are we gonna go?" Pat asked. Weller thought the question over. The fact is, they had a possible clue to Mark's location. In these weather conditions, that clue could easily be lost. However, something didn't feel right inside him. The feel of uneven ground against their boots only intensified that sentiment. Weller knew that the terrain would only get worse as they neared Devil's Rock. They would have to find the Calhoun Trail and take that through the landmark. It was the only trail, as the woods were so thick, it would take an excavation effort just to carve out a new path. With so few people living in the immediate area, the State didn't consider it to be worth the taxpayers' dollars. Even hikers usually strayed from that section of the woods due to the hazardous topography. Even the trees were fighting for space, above and below ground. Several of them had grown far too close to each other. It was practically an overpopulation of forest. Nobody knew why it was called a rock, as it was literally a huge mountain sticking out the side of another mountain.

Weller's hand instinctively moved over his Glock.

"Let's go in a little further," he said. They weaved around a few more trees. Crushed branches marked the ground ahead of them. Some of their fragments were scattered along the trail. As they passed between several more pines, the wind picked up with a deathly howl.

They had reached a patch of forest mostly comprised of horse chestnut trees, whose leaves had been shed for the winter. With nothing but unadorned branches providing an overhead ceiling, the snow had freefallen, burying the ground with inches of white. And with it, the trail had disappeared.

"I say that absolves us," Pat remarked.

"I agree," Weller said. They turned around and started back. The cracking of twigs drew their attention to the left. Weller aimed his flashlight in the direction of the sound.

"See anything?" Pat asked.

"Too many damn trees in the way," Weller said.

"Probably just another branch breaking," Pat said.

"I don't know. Didn't sound like something falling," Weller said. "I'm gonna go have a look."

"Oh, for crying out loud," Pat muttered. He followed Weller along a line of pines. The branches swayed up and down in a constant struggle with the storm. Weller stopped, seeing new prints embedded in the snow. These were deep. Fresh.

Weller took off in a sprint, cupping his hands over his mouth.

"Hello! Sheriff's Office! Is there anyone out there?" Weller called out. Nobody called back.

"He's gotta be here somewhere," Pat said. The tracks were jumbled. There was no order to them. Snow had been tossed about near the tree as though something had moved in a tight circle. The deputies spaced out a few feet as they entered the small clearing. Weller moved to the edge of the tree where the prints disappeared. It rested on the ledge of a hill which sloped down about fifteen feet. He aimed his flashlight down in search of other tracks. There was nothing but a few tree roots and branches intertwined in the snow like sea serpents frozen in combat.

Pat examined the prints in the snow near the tree. The snow had been scooped outward as though something was pushing off against the ground.

The groaning of wood made the hairs on his neck stand on end. In his peripheral vision, he saw a mist of snow rain down. Several branches along the side of the tree bent down like window blinds.

A bulking mass was perched atop of them, its mass weighing down the side of the tree.

Weller started to turn. "I don't know Charlie, you think we ought to—" Weller shrieked as a huge distended bulk descended from the pine tree. Arching legs punched the snow as it landed over Pat, who screamed as it scurried overtop him. Snow blasted through the air in a thick white mist, obscuring the thing from view.

Pat let out a terrified scream which pierced the air, dwarfing the drone of the wind. Weller reached for his Glock and dashed toward the fray, his beam of light zagging back and forth.

Two appendages punched the earth inches ahead of him, bringing him to a halt. The thing turned, its body a disproportionate mass. It was round, but not circular. Its body was segmented, the rear being immensely larger than the front. Numerous appendages, each narrow compared to the body, flicked snow as they turned the head to face Weller.

The front appendages raised high as it started to scurry at him. Weller shrieked and turned to run. His first step was his literal downfall. A tree root, looped about two inches over the ground, had snagged the toe of his boot. Weller reeled forward in a vivid summersault, falling head over heels down the hill. Sticks and branches smashed under his weight, splintering his jacket and skin as he rolled the whole fifteen feet.

He landed on his stomach, his head resting at the foot of the hill. The sound of motion immediately caused him to look upward. Even in his hazed vision, he could see the bending, segmented legs as they carried the creature over the edge of the hill.

Panic struck Weller like lightning, and the instinct of flight kicked into overdrive. There was no other thought in the world now other than escape. He pushed himself to his feet and ran.

# CHAPTER 6

Whimpering with panicked gibberish, the Corporal zigzagged between trees. Even despite the snow, it was the fastest he had ever pushed himself in years. Rapid steps kicked up streams of white mist which sparkled behind him. Branches and bushes cracked as he tore through them like bowling pins. Splinters hung from his jacket, some falling away from the jolt of each step.

The storm, mindless and uncaring, continued its unrelenting assault. Grains of snow, some hard as rock, pelted Weller in the face. He brushed his gloved hand over his eyes, resulting in smearing the snow across his brow, which slid back down over his eyes like sleet. Clumps of snow rained from the trees, showering him as he passed under. Ice frosted at his collar and the wind assaulted his eyes. With every few steps he was bumping into something or tripping over a branch or roots.

Still running blind, he wiped his eyes again. As he did, his left shoulder struck the trunk of a maple, sending him into a wild spin. He threw his arms out to help him steady his balance, then continued running. The only rational thought in his head was to put distance between himself and that horrific thing.

He looked back to see if it was behind him. The night, snow, and trees all worked against him, making anything more than ten feet away invisible. He had lost his flashlight in the fall, leaving him blind in perpetual darkness. He turned back, only to be struck in the face by a baseball-sized clump of snow that fell from the branch of a pine. The snowball broke apart into tiny crystals, now reddened by the gash they had formed over his brow.

Blood and water mixed, spreading all over his face with the push of the wind. Weller threw his hands over his face to clear his eyes again, his body jolting as he blindly ran into a bush. Thorns and twigs tore his jacket and pants as he tore through it, trailing stems and dried leaves.

He uncovered his eyes in time to realize that there were no more trees ahead of him. The air was clear, the sky visible, despite the heavy precipitation. The ground was flat at a slightly downward slope. His feet crunched nothing but snow as he ran.

Then ice, which cracked under his weight.

By the time Weller realized where he was, he was already five feet into the lake. The ice imploded and he fell waist deep into the water. The freezing cold was like electricity, shocking him into this new awareness. He yelled out as he turned around inside the breach he had created in the ice sheet. He started racing to shore, only to find himself doubled over on the edge of the ice sheet. It was about a half-inch thick and rock solid. In his state of confusion and panic, he pushed against it, though it wouldn't give way to his limited strength. This led to him trying to prop himself overtop it. He had gotten up to his knees when the ice cracked again. A moment later, the edge broke apart like a glacier, tipping him back into the water.

Weller, now completely drenched, slashed at the ice like a kraken at a ship. His fists hammered down, cracking the ice and breaking it apart. He yelled out with each hit, feeling his hands bruising near the wrists and pinkies. He ripped through the ice until he was shallow enough to stomp through it.

By the time he got to shore, he was shivering. Water streamed over his eyes from his hair, drawing fresh blood from the gash in his forehead. His arms clamped over his chest and his back scrunched as he staggered from the water line. Despite the cold, his mind was still on the creature. He looked to the woods, trying to pinpoint any moving shapes in the dark. Except every shape he saw was moving, as the wind was assaulting every tree in the forest.

Weller looked to his left and gasped at the sight of an object resting about a hundred feet ahead of him. His thoughts immediately went for the creature. Flashes of its horrible, strangely shaped body flashed in his mind.

He stood inert for several seconds, poised to make another retreat. In those seconds, he kept his eyes locked on the shape. It was steady, unmoving. In fact, it was larger than the creature he encountered…whatever it was.

He stumbled closer to it. Upon a closer viewing, he realized he was looking at a garage. The overhead door was open. A red pickup truck rested inside, facing outward, its hood and windshield now covered in snow.

Twenty yards to the left was the driveway to the cabin. Weller eagerly staggered toward it, fighting against the stiffness in his joints. There were no lights shining from inside.

Barely able to see where he was going, Weller grabbed for his iPhone. Water dripped from the Otterbox as he pulled it free. All that would display was a white screen. In moments, that screen went to black, leaving him once again coated in complete darkness. He fumbled in his other pockets for his keys. They rattled as he fumbled through them with his fingers. He felt the round knob of his miniature flashlight keychain and prayed that it would work. He twisted it, and to his amazement, it lit.

Weller hurried past the garage door and stopped. The sight of several items scattered across the cement floor caught his eye. The passenger door was indented, as though something large had struck against it. Several scrapings marked the wall adjacent to it. And it was that moment that he realized that the garage door wasn't open: it had been torn completely off. He could see the corners of it sticking from the snow several meters away, the grey paint almost blending into the snow.

Weller didn't hesitate too long before deciding to continue to the cabin. His body was starting to feel numb from the cold. His teeth were chattering uncontrollably. At the very least, he needed to get out of the wind.

He stumbled through the snow and made his way to the front entrance. There were two doors, a screen door and a main wood door directly behind it. He opened the screen and raised a fist to knock. His hand connected with the wood. The door swung open, having been left unlatched. Weller waited, tensing with the wind on his back.

"Hello!" he called. He waited for an answer, but none came. With the wind and cold overwhelming, he stepped all the way in and closed the door behind him. Not a single light was on in the house. The air was a little warmer in here than outside, but not by much, causing Weller to believe that the power was out. He confirmed this suspicion as he located a light switch and flicked it, only for nothing to happen.

"Hello!" he called again. "Sheriff's Office! Is anyone home?"

There was a truck in the garage. Odd that it'd be there and nobody be around. This was clearly a vacation home. The walls had the reddish cast of oak wood and were covered with photos and memorabilia of the owner's most successful fishing and hunting trips.

To his right was the kitchen. In the sink were used dishes and silverware. Beside it was a gas stove, which had a pot on an active burner with chili inside. It was black at this point, boiling over the rims. The knob had been left on. Weller switched it off, though embracing the little bit of heat which radiated from it.

He turned to his left and saw the living room area. It was a standard cabin set up, with a rocking chair and couch, and a small entry in the back corner leading into a backroom. Between the living room and kitchen was a stairway that led to the second floor.

Dripping wet, Weller aimed his light onto the couch. A novel was left open face down, its pages crumpling against the cushion. Ahead was the fireplace, which had partially burnt wood inside. He pointed his light above it, seeing the empty gun rack protruding from the wall.

The wind kicked, its drone sounding like a low-pitched scream through the walls. An ice-cold draft hit his back, causing him to turn toward the staircase. A few flakes of snow hurled down the path, which confirmed that there was an opening upstairs.

"Is anyone there?" Weller asked again. He grabbed his Glock and held it close as he slowly ascended the steps. The light from his key chain only caught the outline of the bedroom entrance. With darkness at his back, he kept moving up. His hand and gun shook from both cold and fear. He decided to call out again. "This is Deputy Weller. Is anyone ho—"

A burst of wind tore through with a vengeance, swinging the bedroom door out all the way. It slammed hard against the wall, its echo triggering a nervous jolt from Weller.

"God--!" he stammered. He sucked in a deep breath, watching the white mist enter through the bedroom. He took another step up. The bottom of the door frame was now in view. His light struck the edges of what appeared to be broken fragments of a coffee cup, blown into the hallway by the wind.

Weller came to the top of the stairway and approached the door. Now his pistol was pointed away, his finger resting against the trigger guard. The sheets and blankets flapped in the wind. The contents on the night stand were in shambles. The lamp had fallen over completely and shattered pieces of its lightbulb all over the floor, which were scattered with Mother Nature's assistance.

Weller entered. Directly across the room was the shattered window. He shone his light up at it, the small beam barely illuminating the whole thing. But it was enough for Weller to notice the chipping at the frames. The wood panels were splintered, the bottom one uprooted as though something of significant size had scraped against it.

He slowly moved around the bed, taking each breath calmly to maintain control of the shakes. He aimed his light down below the window. The floor was covered in glass and snow. Between it all was the metal barrel of a Remington 12-guage shotgun. Taking another step around the bedframe, Weller could see the owner's hand clasping the grip.

"Oh, God," Weller said. He hurried around the bed. "Sir! I—" Weller felt bile rising in the back of his throat as he saw the arm lying beside the bed. Strands of meat dangled around the stump where the bicep had been torn from the shoulder. Beneath the window frame were the frozen stains of blood that streamed to the floor.

Weller yelled as he turned and ran down out of the cabin. The air hit hard as he stumbled out onto the front porch. With his pistol still in hand, he ran out. Wind and snow assaulted his senses, causing him to blindly run into the trees. The terrain assaulted his already tattered uniform, spraying cold water with each contact against the pine branches and thorn bushes. Yelling like a madman, he passed through a hundred yards of forest, hitting all sorts of debris with every step.

His foot hit the ridge of a tree root, causing him to tumble forward. He fell between two trees, planting his face in the snow. He pushed up with both hands, filling the muzzle of his gun with snow as he scampered on his hands and knees. He looked up, realizing he was in another clearing.

Blinding lights overtook him and the drone of the wind was overtaken by a blaring siren and horn.

"Holy mother of—"

The spiraling red light flickered into the trees as the ND Highway Patrol SUV swerved to the left, narrowly avoiding the Deputy. Yelling all sorts of curses, the trooper at the wheel fought for control as the car spun out. The tailspin lasted a long five seconds before its front bumper struck a tree, stopping it in place. An airbag ripped from the steering wheel.

"Fuck!" the trooper yelled as it plastered his face.

"Who the hell is that? One of the missing people?" the trooper in the passenger seat asked.

"If he's not, he's gonna wish he was," the driver said. Both troopers stepped out of the vehicle and turned their flashlights onto Weller. Despite the snow and various residue from the forest, they immediately saw the Sheriff's patch on his sleeve. Weller was still on the ground, appearing to be shaking from the cold.

"Holy shit, Sarge, it's one of the deputies."

"I have eyes too, Hosley," the Sergeant said.

Shivering uncontrollably, Weller looked up and saw the Sergeant approaching. Even in the dark, he could see the muscular frame of his broad shoulders and chest. Snow bunched around his dark blue pants and black boots.

"Deputy?" He glanced down and stopped, cautiously watching the Glock in Weller's hand.

"I'm not sure this guy's got all his eggs in his basket," the second trooper, Hosley, said. He had a slight heavyset figure, his meaty neck hugging the collar of his button shirt and jacket.

The Sergeant slowly approached and reached down. He snatched the gun from Weller's grip and handed it off to Hosley.

"Hey buddy, you need medical attention?" He leaned down and lifted the terrified Deputy off the ground. He and Weller locked eyes for a moment. "Well, well. Ron Weller! I'll be damned."

Weller recognized the gruff features on Sergeant Steven Roman's face. His eyes immediately went to the white mark that covered his left temple. Roman's face appeared rigid as though it were made of brick. Snow trickled from the brim of his trooper hat as he looked around.

"Where's your partner? What are you doing out here on foot? Why the hell are you all wet?"

"I…" Weller struggled to speak. He lifted his arm and pointed down the road. "There's something out---" his teeth chattered from overwhelming cold.

"Shit. Let's get him in the backseat," Roman told Hosley. The trooper opened the back-passenger door then reached to the front console and blasted the heat.

"Isn't that the guy you used to work with?" he asked Roman.

"Yes."

"Same guy you were partnered with when you got the, uh…" Hosley ran his finger over his own temple. Roman opened the front door and sat at the steering wheel. Brushing snow from his jacket, he turned back to face Weller.

"What's the story, Deputy? What the hell happened?"

Weller still had his arms scrunched in front of him.

"Lakehouse…down the…road. There's a body…"

"A body?" Hosley said.

"Your Dispatch said you had a partner with you. Where is he?" Roman said. Weller looked at him, then glanced back into the woods. "Oh, you've got to be kidding me." He picked up the radio. "Car One-oh-Eight. We've found one of the deputies on Shop Road. We're gonna need some units down at the lake. We might have a possible homicide."

# CHAPTER 7

By the time the troopers had dug the snow out from around their vehicle, they could see at least a half-dozen flashers slowly approaching from the distance. Over the next twenty minutes, the group of vehicles, comprising of three Sheriff's Department Interceptors and three Highway Patrol SUVs, made their way down Shop Road, eventually reaching the lake.

The law enforcement officers parked their vehicles all over the property lawn as they started investigating. Weller sat in the backseat of Roman's car. He was now drowsy from the exhaustion and the heat. However, his heart still felt as though it was racing. Each time he blinked, the image of that creature flashed in his eyes. His mind went into a whirlwind as he questioned what he saw.

Weller stared out the window at the numerous cops moving in and out of the cabin. He could see lights shining through the windows. Through the open doorway stood Sheriff Stoll. A fifty-year-old cowboy, he waited as Sergeant Roman and Trooper Hosley approached the building.

********

Deputy McCarter stumbled down the stairway, his face pale from seeing the arm. Troopers set up battery-powered lamps in the kitchen and living room area to improve visibility. The breeze from the door was a welcome one, solely because it didn't carry the odor of flesh.

Hosley blew his nose into a handkerchief as he followed Roman inside.

"The power lines are definitely down," Roman said to the Sheriff.

"No sign of the rest of the body?" Stoll asked.

"Nope, but you should see the side of the freaking building." Roman led the way outside. They walked around the corner to the side of the house where the broken window faced out. Flashlights beamed onto a series of strange scratch marks that covered the whole side of the house.

"What the hell did that?" Stoll asked.

"Maybe it's time we asked your friend," Roman said.

"Wait? Where's Ron and Charlie?" McCarter asked.

"Ron's still warming up in the car," Roman said. "We probably saved him from hyperthermia. Guy's all freaking wet."

"We found a breach in the ice over there on the shore," another trooper called out. "Looks like your buddy ran out there and took a swim."

"The guy can run. I've seen him do it," Roman snickered.

"Hold on a sec. You didn't find Charlie?" McCarter asked.

"There was no sign of him," Roman asked. "Weller could barely make out a sentence."

"Son of a bitch," Stoll said. "We've got a lot of priorities at once. Five missing persons, one of them a Deputy, another a sure homicide. In the middle of a winter storm, no less."

"Sheriff, we need to get out and find him!" McCarter said.

"Sheriff will be responsible for preserving the crime scene until the weather lets up," Roman said. "Until it does, we won't be able to get a coroner out here. I'm assuming nobody has been able to make radio contact with your lost Deputy?"

"You'd know if we did," Stoll grumbled.

"My point is that looking for him will be like looking for a needle in a haystack," Roman said. "If I'm gonna know where to look, I'm gonna need to talk to my good ol' pal Ron Weller."

"If he's not in shape, perhaps it's best to…"

"He'll be fine."

McCarter glared at the Sergeant as he walked to the squad car.

"What's his issue?"

"Don't worry about it," Stoll said.

"Do they know each other?"

"It's a long story. One we don't have time for. Come on," Stoll said. They walked back into the house and waited in the living room area.

********

The doubt flooded his mind again. For what seemed like the hundredth time, Weller pictured the huge jointed shape of the lifeform. The memory of its mass scurrying onto Pat replayed on a horrible loop in his mind.

The sound of the door opening snapped Weller into reality. The wind rushed into the car, causing the Corporal to shiver. Sergeant Roman leaned in and snapped his fingers in front of his eyes.

"Wakey, wakey. Time to give us a little debrief, Weller," Roman said to him. The two shared an unfriendly stare for a moment before Weller stepped out of the car. The damp uniform weighed down on him, and the cold hit with a shock against his skin as he walked with Roman into the cabin.

A couple of deputies stumbled down the stairway and out the front door, both of them looking sick from seeing the arm. Holding their stomachs, they dry heaved along the front porch.

"Hey, if you guys are gonna do that, could you take it over there?" Roman called at them over the wind.

"You have a problem, Sergeant?" Sheriff Stoll stepped out from the front door entrance. He stared at Roman with disdain. The Sergeant wasn't bothered by it.

"This is a crime scene and I don't want your puppies barfing all over it. We're probably gonna be here a while, and I don't feel like stepping over it." He pushed Weller from behind. "Hurry it up, hotshot. Time to debrief."

Suddenly, Weller's worn-down expression lit into one of fury. He turned around and shoved Roman back.

"Listen, you jackass…"

"Hey GUYS!" Stoll yelled at them. The trooper and Deputy stood toe-to-toe for a minute, each one harboring contempt for the other. "Ron! Get inside." Weller listened to the Sheriff and stepped inside the cabin. Officers were combing the interior, taking pictures and dusting for fingerprints. He felt a hand touch his shoulder. The Sheriff stood at his side. Snow had frosted in his brown mustache and his skin had paled. "Sit down."

"I *was* sitting down," Weller said, rubbing his hands together and blowing on them.

"Yeah, we're not keen on standing in the wind for story time," Roman said. He stepped in front of him, arms crossed in front of his muscular frame. His uncomfortable presence only added to the tension that Weller was feeling.

"Ron?!" Stoll raised his voice. "Where the hell is Charlie?" Weller tensed as though in pain. It was the question he didn't want to answer. He didn't know what to say. If he described what he saw, or at least what he thought he saw, they'd immediately think he was crazy.

"I... We..." he fumbled for words.

"Something happened and you left him behind?" Roman said. It sounded more like a statement than a question. "Seems plausible. Definitely wouldn't put it out of the realm of possibility for you."

"Fuck you," Weller said.

"Did you guys encounter the owner of the Dodge?" Hosley asked.

"Why did you have your gun drawn?" Roman asked. "You mentioned seeing someone out there when we found you."

"No, not someone. Something," Weller said.

"Some*thing*?" Roman said. He was struggling to suppress a grin.

"Oh, Lord. You guys encountered a mountain lion?" Stoll asked, his face displaying dread. During the past two years, there had been a steady increase in the population of wildcats, particularly mountain lions. With their increase in numbers came a steady incline of reported attacks on hikers.

"No," Weller said. "I...whatever it was it was big. We crossed Boyer Road and found Matt's plow. There were tracks leading into the woods across the street."

"Across the street. Out toward Devil's Rock?" Roman asked.

"The tracks didn't go that far. We lost the trail after a short trek," Weller said.

The Sheriff leaned close. "Ron, what happened? Is Charlie alive?"

"I...don't know," Weller said. "It moved fast. It was big. It was dark. Snow was everywhere. I didn't see exactly what it was."

"I see you didn't stay long enough to help," Roman said. He pulled out Weller's Glock and removed the full magazine. "Not a single round fired."

"I fell down a hill!" Weller said defensively. "It was starting to come after me. I just...I didn't..." He started to stammer as he pictured the huge arching legs and distended body.

"You keep mentioning *it*. What the hell is IT?!" Roman growled.

"I don't fucking know! I didn't really see it!"

"You saw enough to know it got your pal. Or did you," Roman lifted his fingers to form air quotes, "fall down the hill before you saw that too?" Weller shot to his feet.

"That's enough! The both of you!" Stoll shouted.

"You're not gonna be giving me orders, Sheriff," Roman said. "I'm in charge of this. If you wanted to run the show, you should've gotten here earlier. How pathetic is it that we beat most of your personnel to this location?"

"Listen, Sergeant…" Stoll grimaced as he held back on his argument. The Sergeant was not going to listen to the excuses about bad road conditions and numerous incidents in town which slowed him down. It was best to say nothing.

Red lights outside interrupted the tension as another county vehicle pulled up onto the lawn. A single deputy stepped out of the driver's seat and walked up to the house. Stoll knew from the gleeful spring in the deputy's step that it was Jameson. He held a glass carafe in his hand, filled to the brim with black coffee.

"Hey guys! Anyone in the mood for hot Joe?!"

All at once, the officers nearly charged the door for their cup.

"Oh, thank God," Trooper Hosley said. "I guess we can't complain about all you County guys." He took a sip. "I'll be goddamned! It's fresh too!"

"Hell yeah. I got a Roadpro!" Jameson said. He stepped into the cabin, pouring coffee into Styrofoam cups.

"At least one of you guys is on the ball," Roman said. He accepted a cup and let Jameson fill it for him.

"Jameson, thank God you like to spend your money on a bunch of stupid shit," McCarter said. His eyebrows perked up as he recalled Jameson's tendency for overpreparing. "Hey? Did you happen to pack your extra uniform?"

"Yeah. In the trunk. Why?"

"Pop the trunk and let me get it. Weller's freezing. Ask me about it later."

"Okay…" Jameson pulled his fob out of his pocket and popped the trunk, then resumed filling coffee cups.

"Sheriff? Want some?"

Stoll's face was turning red with anger. "Listen! We have a Deputy missing, and you're wasting time with games." Jameson's merry expression transformed into one of shock.

"Wait? Who's missing?"

Sergeant Roman downed his coffee before shooting a hostile glare at the Sheriff.

"I'm aware of that. Considering I'm gonna have to go out there and look for him, I'm doubly aware of it. Since we don't have a tracker handy, you'll be leading the way." He pointed to Weller.

"The hell?"

"You're kidding me, right?" Stoll said.

"You want your Deputy found or not?" Roman said. "Considering the faulty information given to us by the Corporal here, I have to assume we've got ourselves a homicidal maniac out there somewhere. That, or maybe a tree fell on your Deputy. Who the hell knows at this point. But he is missing, and Weller's the last person to see him. But hey, if you insist, we can search again in the morning. Keep in mind, it won't be a pretty sight when we peel him off the ice."

"You'll have dry clothes in a minute. We have extra jackets for you to wear. I know one that should fit," Roman said.

"Sergeant, he's not in any…"

"Sheriff, I'll do it," Weller interrupted him. All eyes looked to the Corporal. "I really don't know if he's still alive. But I owe it to him to go out there and find him." His eyes directed their stare back to Roman. "Even if it means working with you again."

Roman grinned. He turned to look at Jameson.

"You don't have any booze to put in this coffee, do you?"

"Um…no." Jameson felt awkward, unsure whether Roman was joking or not.

# CHAPTER 8

Weller set a flashlight down on the bathroom sink and directed it toward himself in order to see what he was doing.

*Never again will I pick on Jameson*, he thought as he unfolded the uniform shirt and pants. The son of a bitch even carried a spare undershirt. Luckily, they shared the same size.

He shivered as he removed his soaked clothes. He stopped as he stared at his reflection in the mirror, specifically at the pale mark that lined his abdomen. He remembered the sensation of windshield glass slicing his skin. In that memory was the smell of burning fuel, the sound of gunshots, and the sight of blood splattering over the pavement.

There was a dry bath towel folded in the cabinet. Weller took the liberty to pat himself dry with it. Unfortunately, there was no replacement for his socks and boots, though the boots had already just about dried. It was the one advantage of the super cold air. Nothing stayed moist for too long.

As he reached for the clean shirt, he noticed the shakes in his hands, and it wasn't from the cold. The thought of going back in those woods, knowing that thing was out there, made him feel nauseous. Not only that, but it made him question his sanity. Did he really see what he thought he saw? After all, it was dark and there was a lot of snow obscuring his view. Now only that, but it moved so fast. He thought of what else it could've been. Problem was that there weren't many possibilities. There were no grizzlies in this part of the country, and black bears didn't get that big. He thought of Roman's comment about it possibly being an apparition of the forest. Maybe it was possible. It was dark, in high wind, and branches were falling all over the place.

Yet, those legs, so long and outstretched, and that two-part body…there was only one description he could think of. But if he admitted that's what he encountered, even the Sheriff would have him be seen by a psychiatrist. Roman certainly wouldn't entertain the thought of a giant arachnid. Yet, not saying anything would leave the venturing officers unprepared.

The door jolted with several hard knocks.

"Hurry it up, princess! We don't have all night!" Roman called. Weller felt his fists tighten as he mentally asked God why Roman of all people had to be the one taking charge. In that same thought, he prayed they'd be quick in finding Pat.

Weller put his duty belt on and snapped the belt-keepers in place. He didn't appreciate dry clothes as much as this moment. He stepped back into the living room. McCarter was seated on the couch, a dry towel laid out on the table in front of him.

"Here," McCarter handed Weller his Glock. "I got the water out and gave it a quick oiling. It was a rushed job, but it should be serviceable."

"Thanks, man," Weller said. He slammed a fresh magazine into the Glock, chambered a round, then holstered it.

"You sure you're feeling okay enough to go out there?" McCarter asked. Weller inhaled a deep breath and released it slowly.

"I panicked. And I ran. When it came down…" he stopped, still unsure whether to honestly describe what he saw. "Pat's still out there. He's a goofball, but he's a good guy. And I need to find him."

"Well, if it makes you feel better, Jameson and I will be out there with you," McCarter said. Weller simply nodded. It didn't do much to make him feel better, but he appreciated the sentiment.

"Wait!" Jameson said from the kitchen. "I'm going too?"

"Yes," Sheriff Stoll said as he came down onto the steps. He glanced out the window at Roman. "I don't trust that dipstick out there not to screw up this search and pin it on us."

As he spoke, the Sergeant started walking back toward the cabin. The door swung open and Roman entered the house. He immediately looked to Weller.

"Ah, I see you're all nice and clean," he said.

"Why? You looking for a date?" Weller said.

"I see you still think you're clever. Some things haven't changed since you left the Highway Patrol." Roman directed his attention to the Sheriff. "What are the odds we can get some snowmobiles or a canine unit out here?"

"All the way out here? In this weather? Zip," Stoll said. "Besides, that section of the woods is too thick for snowmobiles. They wouldn't be much use to you unless you were searching along the Calhoun Trail. But in the interior? Believe it or not, you'd have an easier time walking."

"Easy for you to say," Roman said. He glanced outside at the five troopers that waited, then at the three deputies. "Alright, if you girls are all set, then let's get this party started. You," he pointed at Jameson, "bring that coffee maker thing."

"All you had to do was ask," Jameson said as he walked outside. He brought his hood over his head as he and McCarter walked outside. Weller started to follow them out, only to be blocked by Roman's hand on the doorframe.

"I'd like to have a quick word," he said. The Sergeant glanced over at Stoll and nudged his head toward the stairwell. Stoll initially shook his head. After witnessing their hostile encounters, he wasn't too keen on leaving them alone.

"Sir, it's alright," Weller said. A huge stream of breath ripped from the Sheriff's nostrils as he sighed and reluctantly went upstairs. Weller took a step back from the Sergeant and crossed his arms. That white scar on his temple seemed to shine in the cold air. The last time they had seen each other, it was bright red, with hints of white from the exposed skull.

"You know, being shot wasn't even the worst part," Roman growled. "It was the freaking painkillers. Turns out I got addicted to them pretty much right off the bat. At first, it only took one Vicodin to alleviate the pain…"

"Aren't we wasting time…"

"Then, after a while, it was two. Then three. Then I realized the pain wasn't just in my skull. It was everywhere, especially when I went without the pills for a couple hours."

"Roman, I didn't fare too well myself," Weller said. "I still remember my car being airborne and the vertigo from flipping twice."

"I recall telling you not to approach the scene," Roman said. "I'm sure you remember why?"

Weller nodded. Most nights, he could hear in the back of his mind the warning of a second vehicle. And with each replay of that memory, he wished he hadn't driven his vehicle toward the armored truck robbery that was in progress. Roman, who was newly promoted to Sergeant at that time, had warned him not to engage yet. But he did, and he sprung the trap like clockwork. The second vehicle, a stolen semi, was waiting around the corner of the next intersection. They knew the layout of that corner of the city, including the heavy construction that was taking place, leaving limited accessibility for the police. The memory of the impact itself was a blur. Rather, he remembered the impact on the pavement after his car flipped, shattering the windshield. The next thing he remembered was the sound of gunshots, and the feeling of arms grabbing his uniform and pulling him through the windshield. He didn't even notice the piece of glass sticking out of his abdomen until he was suddenly dropped. He remembered Roman hitting the ground beside him and lying motionless. His face was red with blood from the bullet that struck his temple. Everything after that was a blank, but Weller was told that he had sprung to his feet and made a mad dash for safety, leaving the supposedly dead Steven Roman behind. Only after the standoff did he learn that the Sergeant was still alive, and that the bullet had only grazed his skull. The robbers were ultimately arrested and brought to justice, though testifying at their trial would be Weller's last act of duty for the North Dakota Highway Patrol. His superiors offered to relocate him, but there was no way he could escape the scrutiny he earned for jumping the gun.

"I remember," Weller answered Roman.

"Good, so bear in mind, you're gonna be following my orders out there," Roman said. "I don't know what's going on around here, but if you cause any kind of screw-up… I don't care if you get lost, or you get one of my men lost, or misdirect us…"

"Why would I…"

"…or run off," Roman emphasized that point, "…you'll end up back where I found you. Only in worse condition. Do we have an understanding?"

Weller glared silently. "Can we go now? I'm sure you realize there's a storm taking place and there are people missing."

Roman snickered, then yanked the door open. Wind gusted into the cabin, carrying snow deep into the kitchen.

The two officers joined the rest of their posse.

"Let's mount up!" Roman said.

# CHAPTER 9

The windshield wipers squeaked against the glass as they swept sheets of snow onto the road. McCarter was at the wheel, squinting for a decent view of the road. All four vehicles crawled up Boyer Road at an excruciatingly slow pace. All that could clearly be seen through the sheets of white was the red flashers from Sergeant Roman's State SUV. Even the taillights were dim in the night air.

"Gosh, have we even made a quarter mile?" Jameson asked from the back seat.

"Barely that…whoa!" He felt the vehicle pitch as it hit a clump of snow. He eased on the accelerator, only to feel the car bump forward, but unable to gain enough traction to continue.

The State vehicle behind him eased to a stop. It wasn't long before the trooper behind its wheel was yelling through the radio.

"*Need a hand digging out?*"

"Negative. Not yet," McCarter answered. He shifted to *reverse* and gunned it, backtracking the Interceptor through the trail it had made. He gunned it forward again, successfully making it through the huge snow barrier.

"*Jeez, careful with that! You almost rear-ended us!*"

"Shouldn't have pulled up so close, dumb shit," McCarter muttered. He listened to the snow crunching under the tires as he drove. In the passenger seat, Weller was quietly staring into the woods. "Hey Ron, are you even gonna be able to find your trail?"

"At this point? Considering how this snow is all coming down, it's hard to tell," Corporal Weller said.

"Perhaps this is a good time to get a fresh pot started," Jameson said. He held up his coffee pot and the jug of water.

"You'll spill that everywhere," Weller said.

"Hey, those State guys are gonna be bitching the minute we set out. At least this'll shut 'em up." He reached over the center console with the car charger. "You mind?"

Weller took it and inserted it into the plug. He leaned back in his seat and listened to the Deputy pour the water in and scoop the grounds. At least the brewing that followed produced a soothing smell. He stared back at the trees and watched as they seemed to roll past the window as though on a conveyor belt. Red and blue flashers glistened over the same two basic images: pines trees waving in the wind and naked leaf trees.

Weller perked his head. Something shifted between two trunks, kicking up a cloud of snow that separated into red sparkles. He lifted his head from the headrest and pressed his forehead against the glass.

"Movement!" he said. McCarter snatched the microphone.

"Stop all motors. I repeat, stop all motors."

The three vehicles eased into a stop. Weller was the first to step out, his feet disappearing under the snow.

"What did you see?!" Roman called from the front car.

"I don't know. I thought I saw something move between the trees," Weller answered. He moved around the back and opened the trunk. Behind him, the backup troopers stepped out of the second Interceptor. The driver, Trooper York, approached Weller with a John Wayne-like swagger to her walk. The badge on her ballcap was quickly obscured by a sheet of snow. She chuckled as she watched Weller snatch up the Remington 870.

"Going all out, I see," she remarked. Weller looked back, seeing Trooper York standing with her arms crossed. Her smile exposed teeth as white as the snow that fell around her. But it wasn't friendliness that she was exhibiting, but rather amusement.

"We don't know what we might encounter in there," Weller said.

"We don't, but something tells me you do," she said. Weller shook his head and approached the tree line.

"Weller, what the hell are you doing?" Roman said.

"Sergeant, I recommend anyone going into the woods be armed with a rifle or shotgun until we…"

"I'm not advising everyone go out there with hair triggers," Roman said. Trooper Hosley approached the woods with a bullhorn. He ran a gloved hand over his face, brushing several snowflakes that got netted in his bushy mustache like bread crumbs. He raised the bullhorn to his lips and blasted his voice into the forest.

"This is the Highway Patrol. We are here to help. If you're in the woods, follow the sound of my voice!"

"You sound like a cartoon character!" one of the other troopers called out. Hosley held up his middle finger to Trooper Holt and Trooper Pino, who stood near York's vehicle. Holt and Pino chuckled in unison. Holt had a skinny build with a towering figure of six-foot-six, a figure that contrasted sharply with Pino's short and stocky build. They were the goofballs of the district, always making fun of the dumbest things. Roman often referred to them as the *Abbott and Costello* of the Highway Patrol.

Trooper Hosley continued announcements from the bullhorn. "I repeat! This is the Highway Patrol. We are here to help. If you're in the woods, follow the sound of my voice!"

"Even with that bullhorn, they'll be lucky to hear you through this!" Weller yelled over the wind. He started marching toward the tree line. "We need to go in and take a look."

He barely completed a single step before he was stopped by Roman's hand on his shoulder.

"Weller, I'm not sure I'm okay with you going in there with that shotgun," Roman said. "Pardon me for saying so, but you're looking a little too anxious."

"There's something out there, Roman!"

"Yeah, and if it's your Deputy, I'd rather you didn't accidentally blow his brains out!" Roman yelled back.

"Oh, give me a break…"

"Quit your bitching. You're staying here. End of argument," Roman said. He glanced over his shoulder at his other troopers with authoritative eyes. "Hosley. Benson, York, you all come with me. Everybody else, wait here!"

"Hey! What about us!" Trooper Pino called out.

"Fine, you and Holt can come along too. The county guys can hold the fort down till we get back."

Benson strutted through the snow from the backseat of Roman's vehicle.

"I knew I should've planned my vacation time for this week," he said.

"Quit being such a girl," York quipped. She walked past Weller and his shotgun. "Don't shoot me when I step out, you hear me, Cowboy?"

"With your tiny figure, I'd be surprised he'd even see you," Hosley quipped.

"Beats your fatass physique," she said. She sniffed and looked back to the Ford Interceptor. "Hey, is that coffee I smell?"

"Are you done?" Roman called back at them. The Troopers quit their banter and followed the Sergeant into the tree line. Hosley continued calling out through the bullhorn. His amplified voice carried in the wind, blending in with the swirling howls that reverberated over the trees.

"Fucking jackass," Weller groaned with frustration and waited near the trunk of the Interceptor. Jameson sat in the backseat with the door open.

"She digs me," he said.

"She's probably crazy enough to," McCarter retorted.

********

The troopers branched out and moved further into the woods. The wind pushed on their backs, flopping their hoods over their heads. The trees swayed and snow swirled like little tornadoes.

"Can't see a damn thing," Pino said.

"Hosley. Call again on that bullhorn," Roman ordered.

"If anyone is out in the woods, please follow the sound of my voice and you will receive emergency attention," Hosley blared. Roman stepped over the trunk of an old fallen tree and examined the snow.

"That damn Deputy's probably losing his mind," he muttered.

"Maybe we should postpone the search till morning," Benson said. The twenty-five-year-old trooper was gritting his teeth from the intense wind and cold.

"That could mean the difference between life and death out here," Roman said. "Keep going. I don't want to rule anything out."

"I'm starting to rule out the chances of that coffee being warm when we get back," Hosley said.

The group moved out quietly. Six flashlights beamed into the dark forest. Dark shadows danced in unison with the wilderness that created them. The wind took on a sound that Roman could only describe as a spiraling scream.

The Sergeant focused his light down to the ground. There were several indentations penetrating the snow. Prints of some sort. Whatever they were, they weren't human.

The snapping of branches drew his attention ahead of him. He aimed his light forward and leaned to the left. The lower branches of a nearby pine tree were moving against the wind, meaning something was pressing up against them.

He grabbed his radio speaker, "Everybody stop!" All troopers halted and looked to their Sergeant as he slowly approached the pine. The branches arched again. There was some sort of mass pressing against the tree.

Roman slowly reached for his holster and pulled his Sig Saur P320. Keeping it pointed at the ground, he took a step to the left, keeping his light on the tree. As he took another step, the branches flipped back. A booming grunt rang out, causing Roman to stagger back in.

He saw the animal's huge black mass charge from behind the tree. Jointed legs bent under its six-foot-high mass as it charged through brush and snow at him.

"Christ!" Roman yelled as he aimed his pistol.

********

Multiple gunshots echoed through the trees all the way to the road.

"Holy shit!" McCarter called out. Weller turned toward the woods, eyes wide as he charged with the shotgun in hand. The other deputies quickly followed, each of them drawing their Glocks as they entered the forest. A half-dozen more shots rang out.

Weller followed the tracks, hopping over obstacles in the terrain every few steps. He held his shotgun at his shoulder with the barrel aimed low. Several pine trees obstructed his path. He ducked his head low and plowed between two of them, yelling as he emerged on the other side.

A collection of yells rang out as the six troopers turned toward him in surprise.

"Whoa! Whoa! Whoa!" York yelled out.

"Hey! Hey!" Holt held his hands out. York reached out and redirected the barrel of Weller's shotgun away from her kneecap.

"I said DON'T shoot me," York said. McCarter and Jameson stepped out from behind the tree. They noticed all the troopers breathing heavily as they calmed from the adrenaline rush they just experienced.

"What the hell happened? We heard gunshots," Weller yelled. A flashlight beamed in his face from twenty feet away. Roman holstered his pistol and motioned for the troopers to space out.

"It's possible we found what attacked you and your buddy," he said. Weller felt a chill run down his spine, and it wasn't from the storm.

"What do you mean?"

"Come take a look," Roman said. With the shotgun at his side, Weller marched in the Sergeant's direction. Most of the troopers had their flashlights aimed on the large black mass that laid in the snow near his feet. One of its legs was bent upward, frozen in a deathly pose. Its body was almost ten feet long, with a huge head that was as long as a car hood.

"Congratulations. You killed a moose!" McCarter called out.

"Listen, smartass, don't get all 'tree-hugger' on me. The bastard charged me," Roman said.

"It just charged out of nowhere?"

"With no freaking hesitation. It might've been confused because of the weather," Roman said.

Weller knelt by its body, observing the bullet holes in its neck from Roman's pistol. The snow near its head absorbed the blood like a sponge, causing the spot to melt into a tiny crater.

"You said whatever attacked you was big," Roman said to Weller. "We're not very far from that plow you found. You said you were attacked by something big. I think we found the culprit."

For a moment, Weller wondered if the Sergeant was correct. Perhaps his eyes played tricks on him. Everything did happen so fast.

Those doubts went away when he noticed a mark near the moose's hind leg. Weller brushed past Roman as he moved to inspect. Two red lacerations stretched over the moose's hip. They were fresh, some of the blood still wet in the fur around it.

"I don't think so."

"You don't think so?" Roman exclaimed. "You yourself said you didn't get a look at whatever it was. You said it was big. Here you go. A big fucking animal, who came at us the way you claim it came at you."

"What attacked us had climbed a tree," Weller argued.

"This thing hung around a tree," Roman said.

"I said it climbed it!" Weller shouted. "Can a moose climb a damn tree?!"

"You said you don't know what you saw," Roman said. "Considering how panicked you were, you probably THOUGHT it climbed a tree, when in fact it sprang from between them."

"No, it wasn't a moose," Weller said, his face red with anger. "Listen, I think this thing was attacked by something."

"What the hell are you talking about?" Roman said.

Roman glanced at the lacerations indifferently and shrugged his shoulder. "Oh, give me a break. It probably got away from a mountain lion. Which would explain why it was so pissed off and charged me."

"I'm telling you, it was no mountain lion," Weller said. "We found these marks all over the place when we were searching for the other missing persons."

"Like a mountain lion couldn't have made those other marks too?" York muttered.

Weller was starting to feel overwhelmed. The freezing cold wasn't helping matters. Everyone looked to him as though he was a mental patient. Even his fellow deputies had a worried expression on their faces.

"Ron, why don't you describe in full detail what you saw," McCarter said. Weller spun to look at him, his eyes displaying the emotion of betrayal. His first instinct was to pull rank and refuse. However, everyone, including the Sergeant was looking for answers. His heart rate quickened with the anxiety of being ganged up on.

"Listen, Deputy," Roman grabbed Weller by the shoulder, "I'm standing here in near blizzard-level conditions looking for your pal. I'm not in the most patient of moods. Now, describe what you saw."

Weller yanked his hand away and stepped back. Glancing at all the troopers and deputies, he realized he was on the spot.

"It looked like, uh," he grimaced, knowing he would not be believed. "It had huge legs that looked segmented. And it had many of them, and they curved out from its body. Its skin didn't look like skin. It looked like a shell, like a crab. Its body was enormous…like a big…I don't know, a, uh…" Finally, he yelled. "UGH! It looked like a huge goddamned spider!"

Roman stared at him, his face scrunched with disbelief. He looked over Weller's shoulder at the other troopers. Lips and cheeks were all wrinkling as each of them struggled to hold in their reaction. Then finally, as though on cue, they all burst into a fit of laughter. Weller glared at each of them, his face tensing with anger and embarrassment.

Roman was almost on his knees, his eyes closed tight as he laughed.

"Oh, Ron! Oh, buddy! Wait till everyone at the station hears this one," he said. Weller took a step toward him.

"I swear I ought to…"

His body jolted to the right as Roman snatched the shotgun from his grasp.

"It's probably best I hold this," he said. "I'm not even sure you're in a suitable state of mind to have that sidearm."

"I'm not crazy," Weller said. "I'm telling you, that's what I saw."

"Yeah, uh-huh. You saw a moose," Roman said. He shined his light around into the woods once more before turning back. "Let's get back to the cars. We'll probably find Deputy Pat in the same area you were attacked by this thing."

"He should stand out like a sore thumb! All we need to do is look for a guy in a silk bag!" Pino laughed.

"On a serious note, if you were attacked by this thing, he's possibly badly injured. So, let's quit wasting time here and go get him."

His face was still bright from the laughter as he started walking to the road. The other troopers followed him, many of them continuing to chuckle as they weaved between the trees.

"Need to go back anyway, Sergeant," Benson laughed.

"What for?"

"Gotta get ourselves some paper towels to smush that spider if we run into it!"

The group burst into another fit of laughter.

"Spider-man. Spider-man. Does whatever a spider can," Hosley sang.

"Oh, stop it," York laughed.

"Okay, fine. How 'bout, 'the itsy-bitsy spider crawled up the water spout'…"

McCarter and Jameson stayed behind, both of them silently staring at Weller. He gazed at the dead moose one last time, studying the bent shape in its legs as it laid in the snow. Weller felt the urge to filibuster about how he was not crazy, that he saw what he saw. But now, hearing himself say it out loud, and seeing the reactions of everyone around him, he wondered if he actually was going crazy. He stared at the warm corpse of the moose. Maybe his mind did play tricks on him. His temples began to throb. The stress and mental exertion had produced a migraine.

McCarter's stare couldn't go unnoticed by Weller. He could see the gears turning in the mind of his follow cop. Even Jameson struggled to hide his concern.

"Come on, let's go find Pat," he muttered. He strutted between them, listening to the chatter from the troopers. As he walked, he hoped that Jameson's coffee was still warm. After all, it was the only decent thing he had going for him tonight.

# CHAPTER 10

The remaining drive was quiet and slow. Hardly a word was spoken between the deputies as they followed Roman's police SUV up Boyer Road to the crash site. Weller stared out the window the entire trip, his red hair waving in the full blast of the heater. He pondered the future of his career from hence forth. One thing was for sure: serious repercussions awaited him one way or another. And if Pat was injured, or worse, his career in law enforcement would be over, and likely he'd be forced to attend psychiatric sessions for his 'delusions'. Adding to the strain in his mind was Pat's uncertain fate. Weller hated himself for running, and now he felt that because of him, Pat was lost all alone in the woods.

By the time they arrived, the snow plow had been smothered with several inches of powder. The SUVs and Interceptor parked to the right. All three drivers left the engines running as everyone stepped out.

"Deputy! More coffee!" York said. Jameson held out the pot and refilled her cup. McCarter approached the plow and knelt down to look through the busted windshield. The interior was completely whitened from gusts of wind continuously blowing snow inside of it.

Sergeant Roman and Trooper Hosley quickly observed the damage. They brushed the snow from the hood and bumper, revealing several indentations. Hosley glanced to Weller, who was waiting near the vehicles.

"There's only one explanation of what could've happened here," he said.

"What's that, Hosley?" Roman said.

"The only thing that could inflict this kind of damage and flip an entire vehicle over like a burger on a grill is…a giant spider!" The troopers started cackling again, including Roman.

"Okay, seriously?" McCarter stood up. "People are missing and you're cracking jokes?"

"The 'small town Deputy' is showing in you," Roman said. "We see this shit all the time. Guys like us have to have a little fun with it, otherwise it'll screw you in the head."

"I think it already has," McCarter said.

Roman ignored the insult and continued looking over the scene. He glanced down at the snow covering the road.

"You know, in my experience of hunting giant spiders," the troopers chuckled again, "I've come to learn of a few patterns. One of which is that they would probably leave a bunch of tracks in the snow if they were here."

"There were tracks leading this way," Weller said, pointing behind him.

"Was there eight of 'em?"

Weller seethed. "They might've been Matt's. Maybe someone else. I don't know."

"Alright. Let's go take a look," Roman said. "Everyone keep your guns handy. We're sure to need them in case we, you know, run into that spider!"

"Oh, shit!" Pino yelled out. He slapped his hand against his side as though frustrated. "I forgot to pack the Nantucket pest control spray!"

"Well, we're screwed! Unless one of you packed a giant fly swatter," Hosley said.

"No. But I know an old lady who swallowed a fly," Benson quipped. The laughter continued as they entered the woods. Roman, cackling with his troopers, let Weller walk ahead of them.

"Which way, Corporal?"

"Over here," Weller said. He walked several meters in, his feet crunching many of the same twigs and branches he stepped on earlier in the evening. His body shook with the distant sound of cracking branches in the far distance. He kept his flashlight aimed at the trees, sparking further chuckles from behind him.

He continued a little further then stopped. In his light was the fallen tree where he had lost his glove. It was completely covered in snow now. He leaned over and brushed off the snow. The glove was still there, the sap substance now completely hardened.

"I suppose you're gonna tell me that's a web and that the spider knocked over this tree," Benson hollered. Again, laughter swept through the group. This time, it was drowned out by the wind.

Weller left the glove where it was and flung himself over the log. The troopers and deputies followed, many of their grins disappearing as they struggled to walk the uneven ground of the forest. The path dipped up, then down, then up again like tidal waves. It made passing through the tight grouping of trees all the more difficult.

Weller stopped again as they arrived at the patch of trees where he and Pat had lost the trail.

Behind him, McCarter was speaking into his radio. "This is the Beeman County Sheriff's Office calling for Deputy Charles Pat. Please respond." It was the tenth time he made the call. With the wind assaulting his ears, he had to press the receiver close to his temple to hear anything.

Weller studied the surrounding area with his flashlight. Roman walked up beside him.

"Is this where it happened?"

"No," Weller said. He turned to the right. "We heard something and went this way." It was hard to pick the exact location in the dark, though the abundance of flashlights did provide an advantage. Snow and pine needles flew through the air and pelted their jackets as the cops followed him between several trees. Weller immediately recognized the line of pines where the attack had occurred. The trees were swaying in the exact same manner as before, their wide bodies clashing with the branches of their neighbors.

"It was here."

Roman flirted with the idea of another spider joke but opted instead to focus on the task of locating Pat. Hosley called his name out with the bullhorn while York, Benson, Holt, and Pino scoured the snow for any possible bodies. Weller stepped over to the edge of the hill where he had fallen and shone his flashlight over the trail of brush he fell through.

"No sign of him," Trooper York said. Her ballcap nearly flew off her head, exposing her black hair tied in a bun. She re-secured it and pulled her hood over it. All sense of humor was starting to drain from the group as they endured the onslaught of the storm.

"How long do you want us to stay out here, Sarge?" Benson asked.

"As long as it takes to find Pat," McCarter said. Roman bit his lip. He wanted to minimize their exposure to the storm. However, the professional in him knew that they were capable of continuing a little further. Each of them had been given thermal layers to wear under their uniforms before coming out here. Plus, he knew hot coffee would await in the cars, thanks to Jameson's good planning. In addition, if it was one of his own people stuck out here, he would want to expend all available resources to have them found.

"How far is it to Devil's Rock?" he asked.

"It's a little less than a mile," Jameson said.

"Out here? In this storm? That's more than a little stroll," Pino complained.

"You won't have to worry about it," Roman said. "You and Holt are gonna wait in the vehicles. I want someone there in the off chance that Deputy Pat, or any of the missing persons turn up."

"Hey, no problem, boss. We've got this," Holt enthusiastically said, giving a mock salute as he and Pino started boastfully following their tracks along the trees.

"Good. While you're there, dig the snow out from around the cars," Roman said. Both troopers looked back at him, their faces now displaying the despair of someone sentenced to hard labor. "What? You think I was gonna let you just sit and drink coffee all night?"

"It would've been nice," Holt said.

"Get outta here," Roman said.

"Alright, fine! If the spider resists arrest, don't expect us to come help!" Pino called out.

"I'm sure we'll manage," Roman said. He walked to the northeast corner of the clearing where McCarter stood. To his relief, there appeared to be somewhat of a path carved out between the trees and brush. Twigs and branches were all over the place. Whether someone had come through in the past and made it, or whether it was due to the storm, he didn't know. Nor did he care. "You're familiar with this area, right?" he asked McCarter.

"Well enough to get us to Devil's Rock and back," McCarter said. "Once we get through this patch of woods, we should be able to find the Calhoun Trail, which'll allow us to pick up the pace."

"Let's get started then," Roman said. McCarter went in first, followed by the Sergeant and the other troopers. York stepped aside and waited for Weller to follow.

"You stayin'?"

Looking around nervously, Weller walked past her into the new trail. York started to follow, only to turn back at the sound of a crunching branch. She aimed her flashlight into the trees. It sounded as though it was ground level, and it didn't sound like something that fell.

The wind was in her eyes and the snow was filling her collar. She glanced over her shoulder and saw the others moving off into the distance. She gave one last look toward the direction of the sound.

"Damn Deputy has my imagination going wild now," she said to herself. She turned around and hustled to catch up with the others.

As they disappeared behind a blockade of trees, another branch cracked. Wood snapped as a huge mass moved down the trunk of a maple tree.

# CHAPTER 11

The group of officers walked for what felt like forever. All the way, they were surrounded by thrashing trees and a whirlwind of snow and ice. The forest threw every obstacle imaginable in their path, slowing their stride every few minutes. But about a half hour later, the wind had finally begun to die down. The snow continued to fall, but no longer was it soaring through the air like a meteorite shower. Finally, the ten-degree weather actually felt like ten degrees and not negative twenty. It was a welcome feeling by every member of the group.

"Ow! Damn it!" Benson yelled. The thud of his body falling onto the snow drew chuckles from his fellow troopers.

"Quit sandbagging, Benson," Roman yelled back. The rookie pulled his foot out from under the branch he had tripped on. It was just one item out of an infinite number of natural debris that had been shaken loose from the trees. He stood up and picked up the six-foot long portion of branch.

"Son of a bitch!" Hosley said, his voice full of fascination. "It's obvious that the spider knows we're on to it. It's breaking off branches and setting traps to keep us off its trail."

"Alright, Hosley, it's getting a little old. After all, we don't know for sure it was a spider," Roman said. He laughed and winked at Weller, who walked near the back of the line with York. The only ones not to share the amusement were the deputies. The Sergeant could see silent words being mouthed by Weller, and he was pretty certain they weren't kind ones. Roman was still chuckling as he turned and continued walking with McCarter up the trail. The terrain was now slightly uphill, though the ground at least wasn't as rough as before.

"We should find the Calhoun Park Trail somewhere up ahead," McCarter said.

"Can't be worse than this," York muttered.

"Won't be much better. I guarantee the snow will be deeper up there," McCarter said.

"I don't get it," Benson said. "Why would he go all the way up here? It doesn't make sense."

"He probably got turned around," Roman said. "If I was pummeled by a moose as big as the one he ran into, I wouldn't know what the hell I was doing either."

Weller seethed. The mention of the moose was a deliberate jab at him. It was a subtle jab, but a jab nonetheless. He felt his heart rate increasing, and it wasn't from the physical exertion. His exasperation was betrayed by the breath rising in the cold air. York took notice and leaned in toward him.

"Just relax," she whispered. "They're just blowing off a little ste—"

"Lady, I don't need you telling me to relax," Weller said in an audible tone. All eyes turned toward them. York stepped away, her hands raised in surrender.

"Hey, you're the one who left your partner behind. Not us," she muttered.

"Get off my case," he said.

"Hey, how 'bout this," Jameson said, attempting to alleviate the mood. "With the storm settling, maybe I can get a signal on my phone and we can listen to the replay of the Vikings game."

"In this weather? Good luck," Benson said.

"I don't know. It's clearing up a bit. I might be able to get a signal," Jameson said.

Weller felt his neurons lighting up as an idea came to mind. He called ahead to McCarter.

"Deputy! Make another call on the radio." McCarter unclipped his transmitter and started another broadcast.

"We've tried it a million times," Hosley said. "The signal's not getting through."

"The storm's dying down," Weller said. "Some of the interference may have lifted."

"Or, you guys just have crappy equipment," Roman said.

"You guys mind?" McCarter said. Roman let out a strong exhale and stood quiet, figuring it would be quicker to let the deputies waste a couple of minutes than to argue. McCarter cupped his hands around the mic. "This is the Beeman County Sheriff's

Department making an emergency transmission for Deputy Charles Pat. Charlie, if you're hearing this, please respond and we'll come and get you." He released the transmitter and waited. Several seconds of silence passed.

"There, satisfied?" Roman said to Weller. "Mind if we move now?"

"Wait!" McCarter called out. Roman listened as a clicking sound came through the receiver. With each click came silence and a very mild static. Rather, it was the same kind of click that came through whenever someone on the frequency pressed the transmitter.

Weller pushed to the front of the group.

"Somebody's doing that," he said.

"You sure it's not just your equipment fouling up?" Roman said.

"Don't think so," McCarter said. He spoke into the transmitter once more, "Deputy Pat? Is that you?" The same clicking continued. McCarter shook his head and looked back at Weller. "It's definitely a transmitter. Don't know whether it's Pat or not. All I can say is that somebody on our frequency is doing this."

"He's probably close," Weller said.

"Why wouldn't he say anything?" Jameson said.

"Probably because he's hurt and freezing to death," Weller muttered. He continued hiking up the path with an increased pace. "You coming? Or would you rather insult me some more?"

"We can do both at once," Roman quipped as he sprinted to catch up. Several of the cops grunted and spat during their hustle to keep up with them.

# CHAPTER 12

"Okay, break time's over," Trooper Holt said. He stepped out of the SUV and with the winter brush, he continued the seemingly relentless task of clearing the vehicles of snow.

"Already?" Pino complained as he stepped out of the passenger seat.

"Look, the wind isn't blowing as hard. Finally. They're probably gonna be back soon, and Roman's gonna wanna take off and leave. I don't care to be on the receiving end of the inevitable shitstorm that'll happen if he sees we've just been sitting on our asses this whole time." He started brushing huge scoops of snow off the SUV's hood.

Pino grabbed the snow shovel out from the back and started scooping out from the passenger side tires. Snow rained down around him in large soft flakes. A small gust of wind stirred them about, then settled again, leaving them to gracefully descend. Their white color turned bright cold as they entered the grace of the SUV's headlights. Like tiny fireflies, they danced in small circles before disappearing into the accumulation below.

Watching the display, Holt found himself looking up at the vehicle in the front of the row.

"You know?" he stopped and sighed. "Shit. We should probably start with the Sarge's car."

"Gosh, you're eager to please. You do realize he's not royalty, right?"

"No, but he'll still get pissed. I'd rather not get on his bad side."

"Why don't you just bend over when he gets here too," Pino joked.

"You're hilarious. If he gets here and we're not done, I'll be sure to let him know it was your idea. That shitstorm's coming either way." Pino tossed another scoop of snow to the side.

"Hey, if you want, go take the shovel from his seat and start scooping away," he said. "I've already gotten started on this." Holt groaned, then thought about it for a moment. Though he hated to admit Pino was right about anything, he couldn't deny it was smarter for them to work on both vehicles at once.

"Don't take too long. The way this stuff is coming down, we'll be using these shovels to unbury ourselves," he said as he walked ahead. Pino continued scooping away, spitting as a sudden gust of wind blew a bunch of snow in his face. Holt smiled as he listened to the numerous curses that followed. "Serves him right," he mumbled.

Holt opened up the trunk to Car 204 and pulled out the snow shovel. He plunged the scoop down into the snow. It lifted, carrying a twenty-pound load that broke apart into a sparkling white mist as he tossed it away. The wind blew again, sending that mist right back at him.

Now Holt was the one cursing and spitting. The snow assaulted the few openings in his jacket as though consciously aiming for them. He dropped the shovel and brushed the particles from his face and collar.

He stopped as he heard Pino slamming one of the car doors. The only reason it even got his attention was the fact that it was the County vehicle he was getting in.

"Luis? What the hell are you doing?"

"Nuttin'!" Pino called back.

"You're getting into that Deputy's coffee machine, aren't ya?!" Holt said. Pino opened the door back up. He had a half-cocked grin on his face, one of somebody caught doing something they shouldn't be.

"Hey, I could use the kick," he said.

"Sneaky shit," Holt muttered under his breath. With his voice now raised, he said, "Make me one too while you're at it." Pino gave him a thumbs-up and dipped back into the Interceptor.

Holt picked the shovel back up and continued clearing the snow from around the SUV's rear tires. It took at least two scoops to break all the way down to the pavement. Instead of throwing the loads into the wind, he threw it into the woods. With each toss, he watched the huge sparkling cloud break apart in the beam of the headlights.

The sound of crackling branches overtook the wind. The sparkling cloud of snow disappeared behind a huge shadow. Holt had plunged the blade near the rear passenger tire and tossed the snow aside. He watched the snow hit something solid and break apart in clumps.

Holt dropped the shovel as he saw the mass approaching. The headlights beamed over its hide, illuminating the light brown color of a rigid exoskeleton. Numerous legs, long and jointed, curved out from its sides. Two eye sacks extended like huge red bulbs from its rounded face. And those eyes were focused on him, while razor sharp appendages, like black daggers over a fleshy mouth, twitched eight inches below them. Tiny drops of watery liquid dripped from their tips.

Its legs arched, holding its body low in a poised position. Terror struck Holt, who let out a scream as he turned to flee. The arachnid pounced off its back legs, while the first four of its eight legs vaulted down at its prey. The first two came down directly in front of Holt like a medieval gate, and in a clawing motion, they scooped him towards its mouth.

Holt jolted back and forth, ultimately spiraling into the creature's face. He screamed again as the daggers protruded from its face like lances.

Coffee splattered over the floor and seat as Pino rushed out of the Interceptor. With snow caked over the windows and windshield, he had been blind to everything outside. The screams which alerted him had ceased with the suddenness of stopping a record player.

"Holt!" he yelled out as he stepped to the front of the vehicle. The headlights illuminated a large trail in the snow, as though a huge boulder had been dragged through. At that moment, he heard the scraping sounds of clawed feet against pavement to his left.

He first saw its enormous abdomen, huge and disproportionately shaped. Legs lifted upward from its side, each one maintaining a curved posture even when elevated. Snow swirled on the ground as it turned around, dragging a limp Trooper Holt in its mandibles. Pino froze in shock and disbelief, the former of which quickly gave way to panic as the beast began to approach.

Yells of a frightened man echoed through the trees. Snow sprayed from branches as the trooper brushed past them. He ran blindly through the woods, hitting obstacles with each step of the way. Only once did he look back, seeing nothing but trees behind him.

The chaotic sounds of the brush behind those trees betrayed its presence.

Pino turned his eyes forward again, just in time to see the tree two feet in front of him. His body bounced off its trunk like a stone cast on a brick wall. He spiraled to the left in a failed attempt to keep his balance, before landing in a snowbank. Blood spilled from the throbbing gash in his forehead and mixed with the snow on his face, creating a red slushy mixture in his eyes. Dazed, yet fueled with adrenaline, he tried to get up. He ran his sleeves over his face to clear his eyes, smearing the blood onto his cheeks and mouth.

His eyes opened to the sight of the approaching arachnid. Pino yelled and grabbed for his pistol. Two shots rang out as it seized him with legs and jowls. The gun flung from his waving arms, which soon fell limp as the venom coursed his veins.

# CHAPTER 13

Insulated boots punched holes in the snow that covered the ten-foot wide space between the trees that made up the Calhoun Trail. The search party waited a moment, catching their breaths while Roman and McCarter worked to decide which way to walk. Weaving through the forest like a gigantic python, the trail stretched what seemed like forever both north and south. At this point, it was a guessing game. There were no tracks on the trail to imply that Pat had been through here.

After a moment of pondering, McCarter took a left turn. If Pat had followed the trail, it was possible that he had come out of the woods further down. If so, they would find his footprints. At least, that was how Weller rationalized it to Roman, and McCarter agreed. Silently, however, he doubted Pat had walked this far. It was becoming a tricky situation. McCarter continued the broadcasts, with no results. Even the mysterious clicking had stopped.

It was a relief to not be maneuvering around trees with nearly every step. For once, the beams from their flashlights could light a path for more than five feet before hitting an obstruction. The ground was relatively flat, though the route would continue to take them on additional uphill climbs. In normal summer hours, it wouldn't have slowed them down at all. But it was the accumulation of snow that made it difficult. And the wind hadn't subsided completely. Though the constant squall had passed over, the weather still packed a punch with residual wind gusts that swept through every few minutes.

The snow was still coming down hard. The group grew exhausted, the troopers now lacking the sense of humor they had employed at Weller's expense. It was the one positive thing about this trip, as far as he was concerned. Along with the physical fatigue and low temperatures came frustration. By now, it seemed likely that this was a wild goose chase. Each of the troopers suspected that Pat had hiked Boyer Road back to where it intersected with the Main Road.

The troopers were glancing at one another, each gaze mirroring a desire to turn back. However, none of them had the nerve to ask Roman. Not to mention, it would certainly spark heated discussion with the deputies. They continued in silence. Yellow streams of lights cut through the woods as they moved along. Weller watched the lights almost unblinkingly, taking his eyes off them just enough to keep track of where he was going. He watched each shape behind those trees with intent.

"Hold up," he said. He stopped and walked to the edge of the trail. The group stopped and watched as he aimed his light deeper into the forest.

"What do you see?" Roman said in an exasperated tone.

"I don't know. There's something," Weller said. He started walking through the trees toward the object in the snow. Roman groaned, then followed. He and Weller walked through thick forest, scratching their jackets against pine branches every few feet. They gathered near the large lump in the snow. Weller brushed the snow off with his hand, exposing chipped yellow paint. It was a snowmobile.

Roman nodded, feeling somewhat impressed that Weller was able to spot this in such thick terrain at night.

"You should be a park ranger," he joked. Twigs snapped on the ground as the rest of the cops gathered. Weller finished brushing the snow off the vehicle. It was in mangled condition. The skis were bent out of proportion. The windshield and headlights had been shattered. One of the ski springs had been completely torn away. The tracks and side rails were intact, but above them, the running board had been smashed and the reflectors shattered.

"It looks like somebody crashed," Jameson said.

"Who'd be dumb enough to try driving off the trail?" York said.

"I'm not sure it's as simple as that," Weller said. He observed that many of the scratch marks were mainly on the right side of the vehicle. "I think this thing has been dragged."

"Oh boy, here it comes," Hosley muttered to himself.

"Dragged by what?" Roman said. "This thing weighs around four hundred pounds. Obviously, you're not suggesting that a person dragged it through the woods. For no reason other than to leave it here, I might add."

Weller stood up from the vehicle.

"No." He pointed his light to the right into a section of forest that appeared spaced out. "But something did go through here."

"Probably another idiot on a snowmobile," Hosley said. "Though…there might be another explanation…" He grinned at Weller. Before he could deliver the punchline, Roman interrupted him.

"How far do you think that goes?"

"If I remember right, there should be a rock bank at the other side of these woods," Weller answered. "It's what's left of a dried-up creek."

"It doesn't make sense why he'd go there," McCarter said.

"Pat might not have gone up there. But, there is someone crazy enough to hack that cabin owner to pieces. He didn't bother to take the shotgun, meaning he's probably got a pattern."

"You think this guy likes to live like some sort of Wildman?" York said.

"A creek, surrounded by woods, would be an ideal spot for someone like that to set up camp if he didn't want to use shelter," Roman said. Weller resisted the urge to shake his head. He still disagreed that it was a person causing these disappearances, but his reasoning would only be met with scorn and mockery.

"That's a bit of a stretch," McCarter said.

"For you or I to be camping up there in winter, it would be," Roman said. "For someone who is crazed out of their mind, not so much." The Sergeant stepped into the small clearing and observed the forest that extended beyond. Watching the snow raining down in the cold night air, he decided that this would be the last place they would look. "We'll check it out. After this, we'll turn back, whether we find anything or not."

"You can go back if you want," Weller said. "I'm not leaving Charlie out here."

"Be my guest," Roman said. "But it's pitch black out. There's a whole world of forest we haven't checked yet. There have been obvious places your pal could've have gone to, but he didn't go there."

"What if we split up to cover more ground?" Benson asked.

"That's probably the dumbest thing we could do right now," Roman said. "Splitting up in this forest at night, during heavy snowfall and with bad radio interference, Rookie, I've seen better logic in a flat-earth theory."

"What about the logic of hunting a psycho killer at night?"

"Considering that numerous people are confirmed missing, I would consider it part of our job description to at least check it out," Roman said.

"Hell, I don't understand why we're standing around talking about it," York said. She stepped around the snowmobile and began trekking the path. "Sooner we get this over with, sooner we can go back."

"Fine with me," Hosley muttered. The rest of the group followed them, leaving Weller and Roman standing eye-to-eye as though on the brink of another confrontation.

"If you have something to say, it's best you keep it to yourself," the Sergeant said.

McCarter stopped and watched the two, focusing mainly on Weller, in case the standoff escalated. Never in the three years he'd known him had he ever seen the Corporal so uneasy. Weller could see him in his peripheral vision. The concern was plain on the Deputy's face. It had been there ever since he saw the moose.

Weller turned away from Roman, kicking the snowmobile in frustration as he started to follow the others. McCarter followed him, his words of luxury falling on deaf ears.

As Sergeant Roman began to follow, he glanced down at the hood of the snowmobile one last time. Two scratch marks lined the metal just inches below the broken windshield. He paused a moment, realizing how identical they were to the ones he had seen on the outside of the cabin. It was an odd coincidence: one that made him suspect that possible answers waited at the end of this path.

# CHAPTER 14

The clouds separated like an enormous grey curtain in the sky, allowing the moon to cast its neon reflection onto Devil's Rock. Despite its name, Devil's Rock was not a rock, but a large mound protruding from the side of the mountain like a huge tumor. At its base was the Silverman Creek, which had stretched for miles from the Missouri River. Over the years, it had dried out from built up sediment which blocked the flow of water, leaving a trail of gravel and dried soot as the only reminder of its existence, much of which had been covered by grass. The creek cut between two sections of thick forest like a knife. Here, the ground was fairly even, except for a hill over on the left side.

Jameson dragged his feet as he walked in the middle of the creek. His knees were killing him by now and his back was aching. McCarter wasn't doing much better. He was feeling just as exhausted, and they still had to walk the whole way back.

"Pino? Holt? How's it going over there, you two?" Roman spoke into his radio. This was the second attempt, and like the first, there was no answer. "Goddamn it."

"Guess your equipment sucks out here too," Weller said.

"That, or those two idiots are goofing off," Roman said. He panned his light over the path ahead. The even ground was coming to an end. The creek was beginning to loop downward along a steep hill which led to another heavy section of trees. He shook his head and exhaled, frustrated. "Okay, I'm calling it." He noticed Weller giving him a hard look. Roman pointed a finger at him. "Consider what I told you back at the snowmobile."

"Consider *this*." Weller raised his middle finger. "We have all this area to cover! He might be out here—"

"Ron, come on man," McCarter said. He approached him, hands raised at shoulder level to insinuate that he meant peace. Weller watched his timid posture as he approached.

"McCarter, I'm fine!"

"No, you're not," McCarter said.

"Okay, maybe I'm not. In case you haven't noticed, Charlie's still out here."

"He's not here," Jameson chimed into the conversation. "These are big woods, man. There's snow everywhere. There's no trail."

"The storm's over. We can push on. If there's new tracks…"

"It's night. It's dark. I'm spent. These guys are spent. The roads are still a nightmare. It'll be late morning before we can organize a proper search," Jameson continued.

"He could be dead by then," Weller said. "Listen, I outrank you. Quit your whining."

"Ron, ugh," McCarter groaned. He was now getting genuinely frustrated. The other troopers were beginning to gather around the argument.

"Hey buddy, I outrank you," Roman said. "I know I said you can stay out here if you wanna, but in reality, if I left your ass out here alone to freeze, I'd be facing all kinds of paperwork I'm not in the mood to sign."

"You heard him," Hosley said. The troopers all started to approach Weller.

"Hosley, leave him be," Roman said. His command went unheard by the slapping of his glove against Weller's shoulder.

"Listen, I'm not joking around anymore. I'm cold, tired, and don't really feel like being out here anymore. So, we can go the easy way, or the hard way. Your choice," Hosley said. "Don't make me take your weapon."

"You might be eager to write Pat off," Weller slapped Hosley's hand away, "I'm not."

"Really? Like you were when you left him to get trampled by that moose back there?"

His smirk disappeared as a punch to the nose knocked the trooper on his back. The rest of the troopers moved in on the Deputy, whose sense of self-preservation caused him to instinctively back up into the tree line.

"Knock it off!" McCarter yelled at them. "Your boy had it coming."

"Ease up!" Roman ordered his troopers. They all stopped and backed away from Weller. "Ron, that's your only freebee."

Hosley jumped to his feet, blood spilling from both nostrils onto his uniform.

"The hell you talking about…"

"Shut up, Hosley," Roman said. "I told you to leave him be." The trooper kicked snow as he marched away, holding his mitten to his nose.

Still standing by the trees, Weller sucked in a deep, calming breath. McCarter approached him while the troopers followed Hosley as he angrily marched into the forest on the opposite side of the creek.

"You alright?" he asked.

"Yeah. Honestly, that was really good stress relief," Weller said. A smile actually broke through. McCarter quietly chuckled along with him.

"Can't say that wasn't a little bit satisfying to watch," he said. He snickered once more, watching his breath fade high into the air.

Roman looked at his watch. It was almost midnight, an hour past shift change. York looked at him and nodded her head at the woods where Hosley marched off.

"Want me to go get him?"

"Give him another minute to cool off," Roman said. "Then we'll get on out of here."

As they waited, Jameson continued walking along the center of the creek, feeling the gravel rustling against his boots under the snow. He turned back, killing the boredom with the same routine. In his boredom he took to guessing the size of each pebble as he ground his feet like a toddler.

Suddenly his foot sank about six inches, causing him to stagger forward.

"Fuck," he grumbled. He noticed the judgmental glances from a couple of the troopers. York chuckled then turned away. He smirked to himself. "She digs me." He felt his boot pressing into something round and hard inside the strange indentation in the creek. Curious, he swept his foot from side to side to dust off the eight inches of snow that had accumulated. He knelt down and dug out the rest with his hand. As he did, he felt the frozen mounds of soil which had formed a ring around the two-foot wide crater. His imagination immediately envisioned a meteor crashing. The solid round object only added to that picture.

He could see it bulging from the snow.

Jameson wrapped his fingers around it and pulled away. As he felt it, he realized it wasn't perfectly round, but rather football-shaped. It broke loose from the ice. Jameson held it up, brushed the remaining grains of snow from it, then shined his flashlight over it. Whatever it was, it was ivory in color. It was nearly broken in two. Only a couple of small strands of the shell-like substance held the two halves together on one side. The edges were jagged like teeth, the insides marked with several scrapes. The material itself seemed to have a leathery texture to it. It even appeared to have a bit of flexibility to it, though it was kept rigid by the snow.

Now, that image of a meteor transformed into the image of something digging out of the ground.

*Almost looks like an…*

"Alright!" Sergeant Roman announced. "York. Let's go get Hosley. Everyone else, let's get ready to head back!" York scampered over lumps of snow to catch up with him. As the two troopers wandered into the hill, the other cops started to gather.

McCarter and Weller stepped away from the tree line. Weller shined his light to the opposite side of the creek, hoping to find any other last-minute clues. However, it appeared he had conceded to delay the search until morning.

Jameson gave one last glance at the object.

*Probably just an old football.* He tossed it back in the hole where he found it and walked away to join the other deputies. A gust of wind kicked up, spilling some of the loose snow back over it.

# CHAPTER 15

"Psychopath son of a bitch," Trooper Hosley grumbled as he paced in the woods. His sleeve was now red from pressing the cuff against his bloody nose. The bleeding had finally stopped, leaving dark crust around his nostrils and upper lip. He wasn't ready to return to the group, as he didn't trust himself not to start another conflict with Weller. He cursed Roman under his breath for not holding Weller accountable for the assault.

He glanced back to make sure he could still see the other officers' flashlights. They swept through the trees repeatedly like a group of lighthouses. Off to the right, he saw two of them starting to march into the woods.

"Hosley! Get your ass back here!" It was Roman's voice echoing through the trees. Hosley scowled in anticipation for the upcoming ass-chewing. He waved his flashlight to reveal his location and took a step to approach.

A loud crack resounded from under his boot. Hosley rolled back on his heel, believing he had stepped on another branch. His light glowed over a large lump in the snow. It was a mass with various seeps, like ripples in its bulk where the snow fell through. Hosley moved his foot out of the way to see what he had stepped on.

The object was yellowish-white in color and elongated. Brushing the snow aside with his boot, Hosley noticed a joint where the object had naturally bent. Brushing snow in the other direction, he located the end of the object. It was cone-shaped. From what he could tell, it was brownish black in color. A hoof.

"The hell?" he turned to the bulk laying near him and studied its size. It was almost seven feet in length and was definitely not part of the forest. He brushed the snow off of and stepped back. It was a near perfect skeleton of an adult moose. Strands of broken down tissue stretched between the bones like saliva. Its angular face was still buried in the snow, though its right eye socket was visible due to the hole in the snow.

Hosley leaned in closer. Some of its body was coated with a light-brown substance. It wasn't skin or muscle, nor did it appear to be any sort of bodily fluid. In fact, most of the substance appeared to have formed outside the body like a glaze, as if this animal had been mummified.

The snow crunched behind him as Roman and York approached. The Sergeant was ready to scold him but held back in realization that Hosley was examining something. Roman stepped beside him and observed the skeleton. After a few moments, he glanced back at Hosley and scoffed. The frustration had returned.

"It is a skeleton," he said. "Animals die. The woods are full of them."

"Sir?" York said. Roman looked past the skeleton where York was standing. She looked back at him with the same bewilderment as Hosley. At her feet was another lump in the snow. Roman walked around the moose and shined his light on the object.

This one was a deer skeleton. Like the moose, the bones were mostly intact, held together by a strange glaze-like substance. He had seen enough dead bodies, both human and animal in his career, and in various stages of decay to know that it wasn't dead skin. He guided his light up past the bones at another lump. Lying next to it was another one about as large as the moose. And next to that one was another.

Roman gazed out into the forest. The twilight reflection of the moon shined down through the trees, lighting the forest floor a neon blue. Skeletal remains lined the ground between the trees. Now, he was suspecting something was out of the ordinary. He was looking at a mass grave of creatures of different size and species.

He ambled through the trees with York and Hosley trailing behind. In every direction, his light shined upon another set of bones. Each lay in a different pose, as though something much bigger tossed them aside. Clearing the edge of a thin fir tree, he saw another corpse. The clawed toes in the feet and the fangs protruding from the jaw indicated that this one was a mountain lion. Like the others, it too was coated in the same substance. Lying just a few feet behind it were the bones of another deer.

Roman stepped around it, the whole time keeping the flashlight on the decayed remains. He moved his light away from it. He quickly stopped at the sight of another corpse laying in the snow. Looking back at him were the empty eyes of a human skull.

Roman froze, his eyes fixed on the skeleton. It was arched back, its head tilted to the left. Ice and sap caked to its legs and ribs, containing a few loose shreds of clothing.

York caught up with him and saw the skeleton, the bones caked in the same substance. She gasped and staggered back, dropping her flashlight in the process. She caught her breath and reached down for it, noticing the glimmers of numerous other flashlights flickering in their direction. Weller, McCarter, Jameson, and Benson were approaching from the creek, each shining their light over the boneyard. They had entered the woods with the intention of checking up on the three troopers, only to discover the mass grave for themselves. Each of them looked at the ground with the same flabbergasted expression.

"Oh…" Jameson muttered as he saw the skull. Thin coats of goo shined from the top of its head, holding thin strands of hair.

Hardly a word was spoken as the group shone their lights across the woods, discovering new remains with each twist and turn. Almost every one of them was fully intact, as though the meat had been vacuumed.

Weller moved to the left past another collection of skeletons. About twenty feet ahead of him, he saw that lumps of snow had been brushed away in a circular formation. Laying against the huge clumps were other scattered remains. And in the center of it was a disc-shaped formation in the ground.

Something in the snow reflected his light. It was oval-shaped, made of metal. He knelt down and dug it out of the snow.

It was a police badge. The back pin had been broken free. The metal itself was covered in scratches, as though it had scraped up against everything in the entire forest. Written in a circular motion were the words, *Beeman County Sheriff's Department.*

"What the hell is that?" Roman asked, pointing at the strange disc in the ground. Whatever it was, it was made out of the same substance that coated the skeletons. Only this configuration was made of a thicker accumulation of it. Weller studied its edges, which stuck out an inch from the ground. One thing was for sure, it wasn't part of the earth.

Weller looked again at the badge.

"Charlie's around here somewhere," he said. Behind him, Trooper Benson was visibly growing unnerved. He kept flashing his light over the numerous skeletons around him.

"Maybe we should get out of here," he said.

"Not yet," McCarter said. "We have new evidence to Charlie's location."

"Yeah, a fucking graveyard," Benson said.

"Shh," Roman hissed at him. He knelt down at the saucer and worked his fingertips along the edges. Over on one end, the glaze had caked onto the ground in thinner strands, while the rest seemed to be separate entirely. Pressing his fingers under the edges, he felt the other side of the disc. It was about two or three inches thick, though very solid. He pushed up on his knees and started to lift. To his surprise, it wasn't very heavy.

The officers watched as it slowly opened like a trap door, the thin strands on the closed end acting like a hinge. Weller helped him lift it all the way, while McCarter and York cautiously reached for their sidearms. The air was filled with tension, as if they expected something to spring at them from the other side of that door.

The disc opened straight out, revealing the mouth of a deep tunnel that arched below the surface. It was a wide tunnel, almost as wide as the disc. It remained upright, leaning back a few inches, yet remaining open without needing to be propped. They shone their lights into the tunnel, seeing walls of dirt that disappeared from sight about eight feet down.

Weller got on his hands and knees and leaned down over the ledge. Immediately, he was hit with a horrible smell that made him arch back.

"Oh!" He coughed several times while catching his breath. In his time in law enforcement and investigating homicides, the only thing he'd ever experienced that produced that smell was rotting flesh.

After sucking in a deep breath, he leaned back down.

"Hello!" he yelled. His voice traveled down the tunnel in an echo, as though it were moving into a different dimension. "Charlie! Are you down there?" He waited and hoped for a response. He lowered his head as far as he could, just enough to keep from falling in. All he could hear was the breeze swirling into the tunnel, generating its own ghostly whispers from within. Or was it somebody's labored breathing? At this point, Weller wasn't sure if his mind was playing games with him or not.

"Damn it. We need to take a look," he said.

"There's no way I'm going down there," Roman said. Weller glanced up and beheld a rare sight. The tough-as-nails Highway Patrol Sergeant watched the tunnel with caution. Weller felt the same way, but still couldn't bring himself to leave without checking.

"Why the hell is there a big tunnel in the middle of Devil's Rock?" Hosley asked. His eyes were locked on the black pit, specifically the edge where it disappeared from view. There were several grooves throughout the floor and walls, as though something big had been in and out repeatedly. Despite his intentions, he couldn't help but keep noticing the various bones in his peripheral vision. Something clearly was living in there.

Weller studied the tunnel once more. Judging by its angle, it appeared he would be able to lower himself down with little assistance. However, on his way back he would have to use something like an ice-axe to climb up. He reached down and felt the dirt walls. Though they were cold, they appeared to be soft enough for something to penetrate.

"You have a knife on ya?" he asked. Roman looked at him as though to try and talk him out of it. Instead, he reached into one of his leg pockets and pulled out a black Gerber knife. Weller accepted it from him and unfolded it. It was a good three-inch blade, which would be more than enough for what he needed it for. He slipped its belt clip next to his own pocket knife, which was close to the same size. After sucking another breath of clean air, he swung his legs around and lowered them into the mouth of the pit.

He skidded down several feet, shaking several grains of dirt loose from the wall. Digging in with his heels, he continued down the slope. After a couple of tense moments, he was at the angle where the tunnel disappeared from the above view. The slope leveled off at a slightly downward angle.

The interior was complete darkness, like the throat of some enormous beast. With his light leading the way, Weller continued inside. In just a few steps, he was completely out of view from up top. The ceiling was at least a foot over his head, and the walls were about eight feet wide. As he continued in deeper, the interior gradually widened.

He was trapped in complete silence, broken only by the breezes that made their way through the mouth of the tunnel. Studying the wall to his left, he noticed the glistening of a wet substance glistening in his light. A thin collection of glaze was stringed along the soil. Some of it was weaved into strange funnel shapes, like husks, the exterior of which had been ripped out. Drips of interior substance had solidified as they hung from the broken flaps, resembling brown icicles. Stuck to it were pieces of foreign material, such as fir and teeth.

His memory flashed to the sticky substance he discovered on the log, and the glove he had abandoned to it.

Weller cautiously moved further in. As he did, the tunnel continued to widen, expanding so much that his light could only capture part of it at a time. Weller watched the wall as he passed by more of the broken husks. Shards of dried sap scattered the ground under them like broken glass. Strewn along with them were hooves, antlers, and other organic remains.

Weller came to a halt as his light passed over a set of work boots and torn clothing, all wet with the sticky substance.

Another breeze entered the tunnel. The wind whooshed, giving off a haunted whispering sound in his ear as it passed by. The breeze died down, leaving the air still and wretched. Yet, a dim whisper still continued deep in the dark belly of the pit. It carried no words or air current. Yet, it carried an ambience of pain. It stopped, leaving the Corporal in dead silence.

Weller froze, his eyes observing the darkness ahead of him. The sound came again, barely audible. It was more of a stunted moan than a whisper. But whatever made it, it was alive.

"You hurt?!" he called out. He moved deeper into the pit, shining his light in every direction. Now, the tunnel was at least twenty feet wide. Rock formations, like boulders were scattered along the floor, and pieces of tree root looped out from the dirt walls. Up ahead, he could see the back wall, which was completely covered in the sap substance. Strands of it dangled from the ceiling, while a pile of discarded husks had been stacked a few feet from the left wall.

Further up on the left was something which appeared to be the opening to another passageway. Weller approached it, his right arm removing his Glock from its holster. He approached and stopped. He was accurate in assessing that it was an opening, but it wasn't for another tunnel. It was a large funnel-shaped structure made of the same kind of substance as all the husks. The glaze was hard, yet flexible, and was made up of several long strands. It was at well over twelve-feet in length and cone-shaped, with an opening that stretched at least eight feet wide.

Weller pointed his Glock and aimed his light into the opening. The inner wall had the same spirally appearance as the outside. It was empty, except for fizzy strands of the substance that protruded from the inner walls. Caught within them were chunks of dirt and rock, as well as a few torn scraps of clothing.

Another stifled moan caused Weller to whip to the right. His light beamed onto the wall and the vase-like husks that were strung to it. These ones were fully intact, each of them embalming some sort of mass.

Weller's stomach churned as he approached one of them. He focused his light on it. The glaze was a funnel shape, like the one at the end of the cave, but smaller. Through the glass-like coating, he could see that it contained a watery substance. Behind it all, were the gooey remains of the victim it contained. Floating about in the substance were pieces of clothing, each of them see through broken down by acid. The face was unrecognizable, as all the flesh had been reduced to a gooey substance.

Others were strung up on the wall beside it. Each one was holding another person inside, all in a state of rapid deterioration. At the end of the line, Weller saw the triangular shaped patch of a police jacket through a coating of glaze.

"Oh, God," he muttered. "Charlie!"

He was strung up inside a funnel, the bottom of which where his feet were entombed was three feet off the ground. Weller failed not to gag when he saw his friend's face. The skin was soggy and wrinkled, like wet tissue paper, barely clinging to Pat's skull. One eye was drooped completely shut, while the other had peeled away entirely. His lips were intact, though hanging outstretched with a rubbery appearance. Like the other shells, he could see through it. The bottom appeared bloated, as though carrying a ton of liquid.

"K—" His mouth hardly moved as he attempted to speak.

"Jesus, Lord above. Pat, I'm gonna get you down," Weller comforted him.

"K—ill, meh." His voice was hardly above a whisper.

Weller moved in and reached out to pull the shell off him. "Hang on, let me get this off…" His fingers pressed against the wet glaze. Despite its rigid appearance, it was actually soft and flexible. It squished inward like a sponge, swishing the watery substance inside. Weller recoiled his arms and stumbled back, his face pale from the appalling sensation. "Ohhhh! Gooodddd!" Weller whimpered.

Pat's mouth opened, and a pained yell escaped what was left of his lungs. With his shortness of breath, the sound was reminiscent of a mild yawn. Bits of saliva and acid material spat from his mouth.

"K—ll, m—". His head slumped to the side. "It's…co—ming…bech." Weller pressed his sleeve over his mouth. Through the glaze, he could see Pat's legs, or rather, the legs of his pants. But they were loose, as though there was no muscle tissue behind them. A black object pressed out from the center of the cocoon. It was the radio, still in the grip of a skeletal hand, the thumb still on the transmitter.

Weller groaned in shock, overwhelmed by the situation and unsure of what to do. It was clear that Charlie's body was being broken down by some sort of dissolving liquid inside the sac. The fact that he was still alive was a miracle, or rather, a misfortune. He knew what Charlie was asking of him. With a trembling hand, he reached again for his holster. His heart was racing. Despite the state that Charlie Pat was in, he wasn't sure if he could bring himself to kill someone.

"WELLER!" Roman's voice echoed from the mouth of the tunnel. "What's happening down there?!"

Weller caught his breath, ignoring the horrible stench. He looked back at the illumination of flashlights beaming into the throat of the lair.

"Hang on, Charlie." He hurried back toward the mouth of the tunnel. "Help! Charlie's here!"

"Oh, jeez!" Roman exclaimed as Weller sprang into view. By now, almost everyone had gathered around the opening. Weller was pale in the face and gasping for breath.

"Ron, what the hell's happening?!" McCarter asked.

"He's back there," Weller said, pointing behind him. "He's in bad…he's…we need to hurry."

"Wait! Slow down! What happened?" Roman said.

"We've got to hurry! That thing will be back."

"I'm not going down there," Hosley muttered. He stepped back, each step faster than the last. Backing up with him was York. She was turning her head back and forth.

McCarter got down on his knees and prepared to haul himself down.

"Wait!" Roman called out, holding out his hand.

"We don't have time to argue about this!" McCarter bickered. Hosley backed up further.

"To hell with that, man," he said.

"Wait!" Roman called out again.

"Jameson, I need your help!" McCarter said.

Roman stood straight up and yelled. "WAIT!" Finally, the group went silent. Roman looked around into the woods. "Listen."

They all heard it now. Whatever it was, it was like the sound of a heavy duffel bag being dragged over a driveway. Everyone started looking out into the dark, trying to determine where it was coming from. Flashlight beams whipped across the trees, the wind causing several branches and shadows to play tricks on them.

Then, a shape began to take form in the twilight.

At first, all they could see was a silhouette. Then, in the blink of an eye, it came into view.

Its bulk was circular, though not perfectly round. From both sides of it were numerous extensions that moved up and down like the oars of a ship. Moving at different intervals, they guided the mass through the snow.

It came into the yellow lights, a large rounded shape guided by the eight arching legs. It was fleshy in appearance, yet hard and rigid.

It turned.

Its body was jointed into two parts, the hind abdomen almost three times the size of the thorax. It was darker too, with the front portion and legs being a lighter brown. The shell almost had a corkscrew shape, especially the disproportioned abdomen, as though it too had been weaved. That, or it was just an aberration at birth.

Two eyes, bulging and fleshy membrane sacks on its head, gazed out into the group. It was such a horrid appearance that nobody noticed the two human-sized glaze bags dragging underneath it.

Nausea and tension gripped the cops.

The stare down, which felt like an eternity, had only lasted but a second. The spider reared up, black fangs lifting from under its mouth, and scuttled for the nearest prey.

The group of cops broke apart.

Hosley staggered backward, struggling to free the Glock 19 from his holster. His screams were high-pitched, as if each was trying to form its own plea. Jointed legs scraped the snow and the spider closed in on him. It reared slightly on its back legs and abdomen, exposing its face entirely. Below those melon-sized eye sacks were its mandibles, huge red pedipalps that appeared as wet and soft as the eyes. Attached to them were black six-inch fangs. Dripping venom from their tips, they extended out like spears.

Its four front legs raised high over him and crested like a tidal wave. In a curling motion, they jolted him into the mouth. Hosley's shouts turned into pained grunts as he was pushed and shoved toward those drooling fangs. They punched into his belly just above the waist.

"Go! Move!" Roman mushed McCarter away from the pit. The spider had turned toward them, dragging a limp Hosley under its head. The cracking of multiple firearms ripped through the air. Succumbing to the chaos, the officers scattered. 9mm rounds hit its shell, only to either ricochet off or break into multiple fragments.

Adrenaline surged through his veins as Weller tried to climb the tunnel. Panic took him, turning his mind into a cyclone of incoherent thoughts. The only rational clear voice in his head told him to get out. He clawed at the soil with his hands, only to lose any progress to the steep angle.

At the mouth of the pit was nothing except the flicker of several passing lights. But his ears didn't miss a beat. The air was consumed with gunfire and endless shouting. Feet hustled through the snow in various locations and distances, producing a chaotic image for his mind's eye. The creature's movements were very distinct. Its many feet hit the earth like drums, coupled with the horrid slithering sound of its body dragging with them.

Collecting his thoughts together, Weller grabbed the two knives from his belt and unfolded them. He backed up a few steps then ran toward the wall. With both knives held high, he jumped. He hammered both fists and plunged the blades into the dirt. It worked. His arms trembled as he lifted himself up. He dug his toes into the wall as best he could to help support his weight. He yanked one knife free and stabbed it into the ground above it. The ground was harder up there, forcing him to twist it and wedge it in.

Just a couple more times and he would be at the ledge.

"Look out! Get around it!" Roman yelled. Twelve feet long from mouth-to-spinner, the arachnid moved speedily. Its legs swung about in a huge blur. It shuffled to the left, then the right, then forward, as though undecided on which human to attack. It scurried to the right like a crab.

York screamed and squeezed the trigger repeatedly. Its body rotated and now its head was pointed directly at her. Its mandibles twitched hungrily and oozed their watery venom. Its thirteen-foot leg-span curled in front of its face as it scampered toward her.

In a wave of panic, she turned and ran. On her second step, her foot failed to lift from the ground as though caught in a beartrap. York hit the ground with a heavy thud, her foot entangled in the ribcage of a deer. She clawed at the snow to pull herself away. A huge shadow obliterated the twilight moon and she felt the huge mass above her.

"NO! NOOOO!" She screamed, as though pleading with the spider. Her body arched as the spears entered her back. Her yell quickly diminished into a groan, then to silence. The venom surged through her veins like a computer virus, paralyzing each muscle and leaving her similar to a vegetative state. Only, she was still conscious.

Her limp body jolted as the spider yanked its fangs free. Its legs kicked up snow as it scurried toward the other officers.

Roman ejected his empty magazine and grabbed for a fresh one. The huge mass approached, its fangs now red with blood. Backpedaling beside him was Jameson. He was screaming in hysterics, his gun wavering as he emptied his magazine.

The creature scuttled then pounced to the left, right onto Benson. Its mass knocked the rookie hard on his back. He kicked and screamed, his body pinned by the arachnid's weight. Its jaws twitched as the sacks pumped venom into the appendages. They scraped together, like a butcher sharpening his knifes, then plunged into his sternum.

Benson's body became rigid as though being hit with electricity. His eyes bulged and his tongue protruded almost entirely out of his mouth, followed by spouts of white foam.

The spider yanked its jaws free, and without hesitation, darted for Roman and Jameson. They split up, with Roman running left and Jameson going right. The spider halted, determining which to chase, and in that same instant, the binary function chose Jameson, and the spider continued.

McCarter and Roman fired off at the beast as it chased the Deputy. The creature, being so large, was impossible to miss. The bullets struck the shell, resounding with a dull sound like a metal hammer slamming on a concrete road. Yet, there was no apparent injury inflicted.

Jameson could hear the dreadful scraping and clawing behind him, drawing closer with each instant. Feeling it closing in, he zagged to the right. He yelled and zagged again to the left, nearly colliding with the open trapdoor. As he did, the spider pounced, narrowly missing him and colliding into the hardened substance.

Weller was there, his elbows digging into the corner of the ledge. He started pulling himself up when he felt the pounding of the earth, as though a freight train was rolling his way. Next, he saw Jameson darting past him, and in that same moment he felt the aftershock of some sort of collision behind him.

He looked back just in time to see the trapdoor falling down on him. It struck hard over his head. The impact shook his body, causing him to lose his grip on the ledge. He fell back into the tunnel, rolling head-over-feet through the arch. His knives and flashlight skidded into the distance, the light growing smaller as it rolled back into the tunnel. He settled on his back, arms and legs outstretched.

# CHAPTER 16

For several seconds, Weller was in the realm between consciousness and unconsciousness. His body felt light as a cloud. His eyes closed, seeing imaginary streaks of light that tempted him into a dreamworld.

*Stay awake, you dumb idiot.*

Weller snapped out of it and sucked in a breath of putrid air, coughing it out almost instantly. He rolled over and pushed up on his hands and knees. He could hear the sound of gunfire, muffled through eight-plus feet of earth. Among that gunfire were the terrified screams of the cops, and the scraping of clawed feet. They pounded the earth in rapid succession, accompanied by the heavy sound of dragging.

Weller stood up, his mind still a daze. The only light around him was the distant reflection from his lost flashlight. He took a step forward, only to bump into the tunnel wall. He had no sense of direction. The gunshots continued from above. He could hear the officers running about. The pounding of feet grew louder and more intense, and with it came a panicked scream.

Then, in the blink of an eye, it all went silent. It was as sudden as hitting a light switch. All he would hear now was his own heavy breathing, which was growing more rapid by the second. Weller looked in the direction of his flashlight and studied the distance. It had rolled ten feet away and was pointing away from him. He ran to it and picked it up. Just moving that distance alone meant that the entrance had to be behind him.

He briefly aimed the light into the belly of the tunnel, catching a glimpse of the weaved nest and cocooned victims. There was no helping them at this point. Weller turned and started for the entrance. He studied the ground with his light in search of the knives. He had felt them dislodge from the ground when he fell but did not see where they had landed.

"Where the fuck did they go?" he muttered in frustration.

He froze and listened to the scraping from above. Just from dragging sounds alone, he knew it was the spider. He couldn't pinpoint its exact location. His best odds for escape would be when it was further away. Problem was it was moving all over the place. It became clear that there was no way he was going to get out unseen.

Weller steadied his breathing and focused his thoughts. He was going to climb out as quickly as possible, lift the door, and make a run for it. It was his best and only option. But he needed those damn knives!

He scoured the tunnel floor until he was almost under the door. There! One of the knifes was laying on its side, almost in the dead center of the path. He snatched it up and started looking for the other. He turned frantically, looking over the wall and the floor, but couldn't find the knife. He debated climbing up with just the one. It would be worth a try. With no time to ponder, he hugged the end wall and started sinking the blade into the dirt.

Heavy steps echoed through the ceiling, sending loose clouds of soil trickling down. The sounds grew heavier. And nearer. Weller stopped and suppressed a gasp, sounding like a wheeze. He pushed himself away from the wall…away from that trapdoor. He slowly stepped back into the throat of the tunnel and listened.

He had no doubt now that it was directly above. It was scurrying, as though moving around in a circle.

Weller took another step, unsure of where to go. His breathing intensified. He could feel his pulse rippling throughout his body, down to his toes. He did not want to move further back. Not back *there*. His exhales were shaky and his teeth began to clench. He watched the angle in the tunnel, hoping it would move away again.

Its clawed feet scraped against a glass-like surface. Weller whimpered and backed away further. The arachnid was opening the door. He aimed the flashlight away and press his thumb against the button on the end of the handle. Nothing happened. The button had been locked in place from the fall.

He could see the tips of the spider's legs reaching into the tunnel. Weller suppressed a panicked yell and ran. In just a few steps he was back in its nest. He twisted on his feet, desperate to find a way out.

Those legs were outstretched. It was moving backwards into the tunnel. Its hind end was bulging through the bend, while its front legs pushed it back. Weller yelped. He couldn't hold the flashlight any longer, as it would give away his presence to the arachnid. He dropped it to the ground and moved to the left wall, near the pile of empty husks. Weller darted around them and wedged himself as far as he could between the shells and the wall without rustling them. Even being knelt down, the pile was barely head-level. The husks were very lightweight. A couple of them fell over, making the pile even shorter.

The flashlight settled after hitting the floor, its light giving the end of the tunnel an orange tint. The illumination was faint, but it was enough so Weller could see the sealed cocoons. Across from them was the large funnel. He swallowed hard, realizing it was less than fifteen feet from him. Wincing hard, he grabbed one of the husks and leaned it up in front of him.

The feet were clawing faster. The spider had cleared the narrower portion of the passageway. It scurried back a few steps at a time, stopped, then scurried back a few steps. Weller peeked from around the husk. He could see the enormous abdomen now. It was lifted off the ground this time, while the spider's head was low to the ground.

There was something dragging against the ground. Its mouth parts clung to the limp body of a trooper. Arms dragged over the head, limp as noodles as the body rippled over the ground. It continued its routine, moving a couple of meters backward, stopping, then moving again.

Weller held his breath as the spider entered the light and stopped. It released the body then turned, as though inspecting the area. Its feet flicked the ground. A panicked Weller gritted bared teeth as though in immense pain as he struggled not to shake. He could feel the husk quivering against him. If the spider saw it, he was dead.

It scurried, disappearing out of the light. He listened to its body scratching back toward the entrance. The clawing grew immensely louder as it made its way up and out. Weller hoped that it was gone, but alas, he could already hear it coming back.

Even compared to the surrounding air, the smell from the husk was repugnant. He had to hold it closer to help obscure him from view. He saw the abdomen as the spider entered the wider portion of the lair. The scraping of its victim against the floor echoed in the dark cave. It entered the light and released the next Deputy.

Weller could see from the ballcap that this one was Trooper York. Her body settled with her face turned toward him. Her eyes were frozen open, her jaw slack, as though trying to scream. The spider stood in place above its prizes. It was unmoving, as though trying to detect something. Some of its legs slowly raised, then lowered back down, as though sensitive to touch.

Finally, it scurried toward the entrance again, leaving the two troopers in the light. Weller couldn't help but wait in dead silence, the whole time staring at them. The silence was filled by another moan from Charlie. Weller's stomach churned again. Every sense of his was being assaulted. The grotesque sights of the victims, the horrible sounds, the repugnant smells, the slippery leathery feel of the husk. The air was so thick and so disgusting, he could almost taste it.

They were like statues of deceased knights in their resting place, except there was nothing holy about their demise. He studied them, curious if they were still alive. Then he remembered Charlie. He was still alive, which meant, they had to still be alive. He thought of rushing out to grab them and hiding them near the husks. But would it know? Was it intelligent enough to realize they were missing? It had memory enough to know it had food waiting outside that needed to be brought in. Considering this, Weller realized hiding them would probably entice the spider to search, and inevitably find *him* in the process.

He watched the bodies. Their hands were laid at their sides. Weller coughed as he saw the fingers on York's hand twitching. Either it was a side effect, or she was alive, fighting against the paralysis.

It came back with another trooper in tow. Its body rubbed against the walls as its legs pushed it backward. This time, its movements were slower. Weller brought the husk back over his face, still able to see from around the edge of it. He could see the uniform from the trooper it carried, though he couldn't identify who it was.

But there was something else too. Two long stringy substances were extended from its mandibles. When in the light, they glistened into a light brown, like the glaze that covered the husks. They were as taut as fishing wire, only bending when the arachnid came to a stop. It dropped the trooper and used its front legs to reel in the strings.

Whatever was at the end of them abraded against the tunnel floor. They dragged past the pile of husks into the light. They were two brown bags, weaved in spirals…cocoons. They were almost equal in length to the troopers. Then Weller noticed the open ends, exposing the faces of Pino and Holt. Like York, their faces were frozen with the horror they felt in the moment they were stung.

The spider rustled about between the walls. It inched back and forth, rotating in place as though standing on an album. Its legs, while enormous, appeared skinny compared to the arachnid's bulky shape. Its abdomen had a bumpy design, as though molded from clay. It had several deep indentations in some spots between the spirals, while containing large bumps in other sections. It was a sickly shape.

Finally, it crawled over to the wall between the husk pile and the funnel. It scooted one of the cocooned troopers with its legs, rolling it along with it until at the foot of the wall. It reared back, pushing against the wall with two of its front legs. With the next pair, it lifted the cocoon several feet high.

With its head propped up, the spider angled its abdomen toward the wall until the underside was almost facing upward. In that moment, it resembled a wasp that was ready to sting. But instead of a barb, there was a spinneret protruding from its abdomen. Its back legs kept it balanced while the next pair strung a fresh wet sticky substance from the pore. It was like a typical web like what he had seen on the *Discovery Channel*. But unlike typical spiders, this web was covered in the brown dripping substance that looked like fresh honey. The spider covered the silk bag in the substance, gluing it to the wall behind it. In the opening was Pino's head, now slumped to the side. With the cocoon properly secured, the spider straightened out its body. Then it leaned up closer to it.

Weller shivered as he watched the jaws expand out, forming a V-shape over its mouth. Extending out between the fangs, a wet tube-like appendage reached out. In the dim light, it appeared pink in color, with a circular opening at the end. It touched Pino's face before moving out over the top of his head. From its opening came a watery substance that sprayed as if out of a garden hose. After thoroughly saturating him, the spider withdrew, leaving Pino strung up against the wall. It leaned on its front legs, raising its abdomen high as it backed up toward the others. With one of its inner pair of legs, it scooped up Holt's cocoon and dragged him back and placed him on the wall next to Pino. After plastering him with more of the brown fluid, it applied the watery substance from the fleshy proboscis.

Weller squeezed his eyes shut after hearing another grunt from Pat. It was like that of an animal stirring from slumber.

The spider lowered itself from the wall and backed up again. This time, it turned around completely. It crawled over the troopers to the opposite wall. Again, it reared itself up. Its front legs dug at the empty husks near the sealed cocoons. Like a cat pawing a string, it stroked them until they broke free from the wall. They fell to the ground, spilling residue into the dirt.

It collected them in its mandibles and turned.

Weller's mouth opened to scream as he saw the spider face his direction and stop. He tightened his stomach as he suppressed it. All that came out was hot breath. The light bouncing down from the ceiling reflected those big wet eye-sacks and red tube-shaped jaws containing the fangs. Its legs carried it forward, moving up and down like boat paddles.

Weller slowly sank as low as possible, inching the husk over his face. The pile moved, pressing him against the wall. The legs scratched the ground on the other side. Weller held his breath, feeling every shift in the husks. It rustled the pile as it added the empty cocoons to it. And then, it stood again. Weller didn't move a muscle. He was a mere six feet away from those fangs. He couldn't see it now. He wouldn't dare. He sat on his knees in silence with rotting balm pressing against his face.

The spider crab-walked to its right in a semi-circular path. By the time Weller allowed himself to peek at it again, it was standing once again over the troopers. It reared back and readjusted the huge abdomen to face the underside up. It used the claws on its front legs to snag York by the pantleg and lift her up. With the next pair of legs, it drew the web from its spinneret and bonded it with her midsection. Then, it spun her like a rotisserie, using the motion to draw more of the web out. Adjusting her side to side, it encompassed her with the sticky substance, leaving only her head partly exposed.

It placed her down then snagged one of the other troopers. The fresh silk and its sap produced a fresh smell as it was strung from the abdomen. The spider's jaws nestled together as it completely embalmed its prey. Setting him down, it repeated the same process with the third one. Soon, all three cops were almost completely invisible under the glaze covering.

The spider straightened its posture, then one-by-one, it dragged the three cocoons to the wall where it had cleared the empty husks. As it did with Pino and Holt, it pasted each cocoon to the wall. From across the tunnel, Weller could see its outstretched body in full form as it leaned up against the wall. He couldn't take his eyes off its disgusting abdomen. It was so unbalanced...so strangely shaped, it was nauseating to look at. The corkscrew design of its outer shell only added to the appalling appearance.

With its tongue-like proboscis, it saturated the three cops with the water substance. Whatever it was, it was different than the sap.

Weller glanced at Pat and the cocoons strung up beside him, then closed his eyes in despair. It became obvious that it was a digestive compound to break down its food, which would them be stored in the cocoon for when the spider was ready.

Its legs curled as it lowered itself from the wall. It rustled the ground as it moved back and forth. Slowly, it crawled to the huge funnel it had weaved in the corner. With its legs, it tended to the edges as though conducting maintenance. It dipped its head inside and scraped with its front legs. Its huge abdomen stuck out of the opening, propping up on its end as the spider pulled a few strings of silk to coat the inside.

Weller watched as it leaned back and forth. Its back legs arched around the mouth as though hugging the funnel. Again, Weller felt himself succumbing to the terror of being trapped alive in this lair. He contemplated making a run for the entrance while the spider was in its funnel. A silent debate took place in his mind. Logically, if he ran, he would undoubtedly alert the spider to his presence. And there was no doubt it would close in on him before he could make the climb. But how long could he stay here undetected? Was it going to stay? Would it go back out and hunt?

If so, for how long? If not, for how long? And what the hell was it going to do with the husks?

His eagerness was starting to get the better of him. It almost felt as though his legs were pushing up involuntarily, as if his body was taking full control. The urge to flee was overwhelming. Weller was almost standing straight up now. He raised his foot to take the next step.

The legs twitched as the spider began to back itself out. Weller quivered and lowered himself down. As quietly as he could, he lifted one of the husks to once again block himself from view. The spider fully backed from the funnel and stopped.

Weller's fingers were twitching. He felt his bowels ready to shift and his bladder about to unload. He watched the arachnid as it stood. He wondered if it sensed his movements. It turned again slowly until it faced the other wall. Nestling its fangs, it moved up toward one of the cocoons. Its tube-like mouth extended from between the fangs. Using its legs, it sprawled up over the cocoon.

The Corporal turned pale as he listened to the slurping sounds of it gulping the dissolved contents of that cocoon. It was like an air hose with watery obstructions inside. Its body pulsed as it absorbed the liquid contents. After a few seconds, the slurping stopped and the tunnel momentarily went silent. The spider backed away, leaving a human skull protruding from the otherwise empty cocoon.

A pained grunt ended the silence. Weller wanted to sob, but he couldn't. Pat was still awake, and though he was blind, it was obvious he could sense the spider's presence. Its legs jostled his cocoon as it moved up onto the cocoon next to him. It dipped the pink tube deep into the opening and drained the cocoon of its contents. Like a deflating balloon, the sides of the husk crumpled a few inches inward. The spider pulled away, releasing a small hiss as it withdrew its proboscis. It backed away from the now empty husk and slowly moved to its left.

Pat, through closed jaws, let out another grunt. His head was slumped to the right. Through minor twitches, it was clear he knew that the spider was approaching. From behind the husks, Weller watched in horror as it slowly approached his friend.

*No…no…*

His thoughts evolved into whispers.

"No…no, he's not dead yet…" He heard his own words and cupped his hand over his mouth. Air hissed between his fingers as he felt himself starting to scream.

The spider sprawled over Pat. The grunts were rapid now, possibly from hyperventilating. The spider leaned against him. The tube extended from its ugly head and brushed against Pat's face.

Weller leaned back against the wall in utter horror as he bore witness to the feeding.

Pat let out several freaked grunts as the proboscis lowered to his collar. Then the suction began, generating a slurpy sound. Pat's grunt elevated into a pained, bubbly scream as his gooey flesh was vacuumed from his bones. The spider backed away from the husk, leaving a skeleton red with tendons and undigested blood and muscle strands.

Weller grew very light-headed. He wobbled back and forth on his knees, fighting to keep from passing out. *Remember, fall asleep and you'll die!* The spider, satisfyingly nourished, went to work ripping the husks open. Wet substance trickled from the flaps as the claws ripped them down the middle. With its legs, it pulled the skeletons free and dragged them out into the neck of the tunnel. Weller could hear the echoes of scraping claws as it moved up the bend and out of the tunnel. The silence only lasted a few moments as it discarded the unwanted remains.

It crept back into the lair, its legs brushing against the husk pile as it moved toward the funnel. Its legs scrunched together, almost as though it were trying to form a giant fist. Squeezing its body tight, it burrowed into the funnel.

Weller could see the back of its abdomen resting just inside the opening. Two of its back legs protruded alongside it, slowly waving up and down like octopus tentacles. Otherwise, the arachnid was perfectly still.

With the husk still concealing him, Weller waited and watched. He was afraid to move without alerting it.

He was trapped.

# CHAPTER 17

Minutes moved like hours as Weller stared unblinking at the slumbering beast. He had no way of knowing how much time had elapsed, nor was he fully convinced the thing was truly asleep. But there was no way to know.

Weller noticed that the lair was starting to darken. The flashlight was slowly dying. Somehow, the prospect of being blind to the horror around him was worse than actually seeing it. Weller knew that his imagination would run away with every sound he would hear.

It was too much on him. He was trapped in a tunnel with a horrible man-eater. He just wanted it to end. He ran his thumb along the grip of his pistol. In his mind, he envisioned pressing the muzzle to his temple. Just one quick *bang* and it would all be over.

Weller slowly pulled the Glock out and imitated his vision. Somehow, the gun seemed heavier than usual. He felt the circular muzzle crushing his sideburns. His index finger entered the trigger guard. Yet, he couldn't do it. For reasons he couldn't fathom, his finger would not squeeze that trigger and put him out of this horrible nightmare.

He was paralyzed with fear. He desperately wanted to run, but his mind was convinced that any movement would cause the arachnid to stir. The memory flashed of it lunging at him during their first encounter. The only thing that kept him from being snatched in its fangs was the tree root he tripped over and the slope of the hill on which he fell. The distance it instantly put between him and the beast had been his salvation: a literal gift from nature. Or God Himself.

He looked up at the troopers. Even from where he was, he could see that the texture of their skin was changing. The digestive substance was going to work. In that moment, he remembered that they were still alive. Could they feel what was happening? If so, it had to be an unbearable pain. He prayed that they were unconscious. Though, he suspected they weren't.

At that moment, he chose his fate. Witnessing their fates was horrible enough. Weller vowed not to experience it for himself. This species was cruel. It didn't kill its victims and devour them. It stung them and left them to be digested alive. And the same would happen to him if he didn't take action.

The light continued to weaken. Already, Weller could no longer make out the cocoons across from him. Nor could he see the tunnel where the spider slept. In about a minute or so, he would be blind. Already, he was having trouble identifying his surroundings. If he tried to move around this husk pile in black air, he would certainly knock some of them over. He would need some visibility. If he was going to move, it had to be now. And he already knew he wasn't willing to blow his brains out instead. Thus, the choice was clear.

Weller placed the Glock back into the holster and stood straight up. He slowly pressed his hand on the husk that leaned against him and lowered it to the floor. He stepped over it, carefully planting his feet on the other side. There were no sounds coming from the funnel, indicating that the spider didn't move.

The tunnel continued to darken. Weller had to move fast. And with how the pile was pressed into the wall, he had to walk *toward* the spider to get around it.

He stepped over another husk that was lying flat on the ground. He tried to walk quickly while keeping each movement silent. After a few steps, he was at the edge of the pile nearest to the spider. Now he could see it. The abdomen was in the exact same place as before, the legs slowly wriggling beside it.

His foot bumped against a husk. It moved a few inches back, rustling against the dirt.

*Shit!*

Weller lowered into a sprinting position and prepared to take off. To his relief, the spider didn't awaken. He continued to move around the pile until finally he was moving away from the funnel. The timing was perfect, as the flashlight had gone completely dead.

Weller turned to face the other side of the tunnel. He walked in complete darkness, carefully placing each step quietly. After a few steps, he was already starting to feel unbalanced. The physical dizziness played havoc on his mind. He wanted to make a mad dash for freedom.

*No, you'll wake it.*

His body shook as he bumped against the wall, scraping the remnants of a cocoon. Crystalized pieces of sap crunched under his boots. He moved to the right to make some distance from the wall. Instinctively, he looked over his shoulder, despite knowing he would not see it through the dark. The blindness was driving him wild. He might as well be walking with his eyes closed.

He stopped, remembering something. His keys! He shoved his hand into his pocket and thumbed through his keychains, eventually finding the knob of his mini-flashlight. He slowly removed the keys from his pocket, cautiously keeping them from rattling as he removed the ring to the flashlight. Holding the two-and-a-half-inch long flashlight in his hand, he placed the keys back into his pocket. He took several more steps, debating when to risk turning it on.

The light would be small, but enough to help him see what he was doing. However, he worried it might attract the spider. From its perception, a moving light would indicate the presence of something to eat. But the fact remained that he needed to turn it on at some point. The spider was facing away from him, after all.

"Fuck it," he muttered.

He twisted the knob. A little white stream of light hit the floor. Again, Weller looked behind him. And again, he couldn't see the spider. He did see the tunnel walls, however, and it was enough for him to gauge the distance he had made. He felt confident enough to go faster.

The white light bounced off shards of dried sap on the ceiling. Fragments of glaze reflected from the black floor, resembling stars in a night sky. The walls seemed to get closer together as he continued. He could feel the ground elevating into a slope. He had reached the bend.

So close!

Weller grabbed the knife from his pocket and hurried toward the wall. He pointed the light down for the other one. The spot of white moved across the black floor, finding nothing but gravel and dirt.

A scraping sound echoed from behind him. Weller whipped back and looked into the darkness. He stood completely still and listened. Hearing nothing else, he resumed his search. Another scrape echoed. And another. No doubt, the thing was backing out of its funnel.

Panic hit Weller, driving him to attempt the climb with only the one knife. He flung himself at the wall and plunged the blade into the dirt. He pulled himself up and reached with the other hand. He clawed his fingers into the dirt, trying his best to keep a hold. His whole body trembled as gravity pulled down on him. He yanked the blade out to get the next hold. As soon as it left the groove, Weller fell down, unable to hold on. He hit the tunnel floor and bounced.

The clawing intensified. Now, the spider was undoubtedly aware of his presence.

Weller sprang to his feet, thinking hard on what to do. There was no notch or ledge for him to grab while retracting the knife. Without a second instrument, he would just continue to fall. And the second knife was lost somewhere in the tunnel. Weller looked at his trembling hands and the tools they held. All he had was Roman's knife and the keychain.

*Keychain...keys.*

Weller shoved his hand into his pocket and grabbed the keys. He held the group in a tight wad, letting the one-and-a-half-inch car key stick out like the blade of a knife. He could hear the spider moving through the tunnel.

Weller yelled and threw himself again at the wall, plunging the knife and key into the dirt high over his head. He pulled himself up, scraping his feet below in a bicycle motion. He pulled the knife out to make another plunge. To his relief, the keys held...barely. Wedging the knife into a new notch, he pulled himself higher. The lid was close by now. He reached up again. His hand brushed against the flat end of the disc.

He raked the knife into the wall and twisted it until it sank a couple of inches. Yelling like a crazed lunatic, he hauled himself up and threw his other arm into the door. It lifted up, resting down on his arm as he reached through the gap.

Now the spider was hissing. It was in the narrow portion of the tunnel. Its shell scraped against the roof and its legs extended along the ground beneath Weller's feet.

He yelled out in hysterics and threw his other arm over the edge of the opening. Clawing the snow like a feral cat, he wrenched himself from the pit with the door resting on his back. Finally, everything from the waist up was over the ledge. Weller lifted his legs up until his knees were on the corner.

The spider was coming up through the bend. He felt his foot bounce as its claw grazed the heel of his boot. Weller threw himself forward into a summersault, clearing the trap door in the process. The door flopped shut behind him, only to burst open by a fury of uncurling legs.

After rolling to his feet, Weller turned toward the monster with his Glock drawn. He fired in rapid succession, emptying sixteen of the seventeen rounds. Each one struck the spider, only to crunch against its exoskeleton. It hissed as it began to lift its abdomen. Its legs curled tight around its body, preparing to spring at its prey.

Weller fired the final round. The bullet creased the cold winter air and plunged into the soft rubbery flesh of one of its pedipalps. The spider screeched and reeled back under the trap door in a single reactionary motion, slamming the entrance down over it. Even from above, the echoes of its wild scraping and clawing could be heard.

Ejecting the empty mag, Weller turned and ran for his life. All at once, the combined horror of everything he witnessed and was currently experiencing was released in a rant.

"OH LORD! OH MY GOD! JESUS HEAVEN AND MARY! OH GOD!"

He ran through the trees, passing through the boneyard. As he started down the incline of a hill, he heard the trap door burst open again, followed by another hiss from the spider.

Winding between the trees, Weller pushed himself to his limits. The wind kicked up, throwing snow and ice in his face.

"OH GOD! OH CHRIST! OH—AGH!"

Weller tripped over a branch, sending himself tumbling several feet forward. He rolled over his shoulder and back, settling face down in the snow.

Several footsteps punched the snow, rapidly drawing nearer. Weller pushed up with his hands and desperately started to crawl. He let out another shriek as the feet set down directly beside him.

His jacket tightened near the shoulders from a tight grip and in that same moment he was lifted off the ground. His mind in a frenzy he whipped back with his empty pistol, striking something solid.

"Oh, FUCK!" Roman yelled. The Sergeant staggered back. His hands released Weller's jacket and cupped around his eyebrow. "You damn cocksucker!"

"Roman!" Weller said.

"How the hell did you get out? I thought you were dead!"

"Jesus, Mary, and Joseph, man! You don't wanna know!" He glanced back over his trail. Behind the wall of trees, they could hear the huge mass dragging through the snow. "It's coming! We gotta go!"

# CHAPTER 18

Hot vapor spewed from their mouths as Weller and Roman tore through the forest. The wind swirled around them, making the exposed skin on their faces and Weller's hands cold as ice. They were going in what felt like a random direction. There was no destination other than what was away from the creature.

The snapping of low branches and splashing of snow filled their ears. Weller looked back over his shoulder. He saw nothing but a world of trees and snow, glowing a whiteish-blue in the clear sky. He couldn't see the spider.

But it was there. He could hear its movements and feel its presence. And those movements were gradually growing louder.

Both cops were running out of breath. Large strands of saliva spat from Roman's mouth. His lungs felt like they were turning to stone. Weller was even more exhausted. Even the will to survive couldn't overcome the need to slow down.

"Roman, we're not gonna be able to outrun it," he said. His voice came out as one big wheeze. His throat was dry, his legs becoming like jelly, and his heart felt like it would explode any minute.

Spitting again, Roman glanced back, listening to the spider's frenzied approach.

"We stop, and we'll end up like the others," he said.

"We keep running, we'll end up like the others," Weller said. "That thing can hear every step we make! It'll track us… get your phone out!"

Roman glanced back at him with a puzzled expression. "What? I can't make a call. There's no signal out here!"

"No! You have music downloaded! Turn it on and blast the volume!"

They continued running as Roman fumbled to get the phone off of the belt clip. He yanked the glove off his left hand to operate the touch screen. A white light shined from the button and he got on his downloaded files.

"Think the spider has a preference?" he joked. Weller wasn't amused. Roman hit a button, blasting *Clearance Clearwater Revival*. They ran a little further in search of a good place to hide. Seeing a large collection of thick bushes, he dug his heels into the snow and threw his hands out, warning Roman to stop.

"Throw it that way!" Weller pointed out to a section of woods where the trees were spaced out. Roman took precaution in his aim. If he accidentally broke the phone against a tree, that would render the distraction useless. The phone's light flickered like a shooting star as he launched it into the night. As soon as it left his hand, Weller grabbed him by the shoulder and led him behind the brush.

They leaned down, both gripping freshly loaded sidearms as they waited. The music blasted off beyond the trees to their right. Through the stems of the brush they could see the glint of the touchscreen radiating from the snow.

Up ahead to the left came the swaying of low pines and the snapping of fallen branches. The cops forced their breathing into deep silent breaths through their noses, as the heavy panting from running was too audible. They could see branches beginning to shift outward and spring back as something passed by.

Both men swallowed hard as the arachnid emerged between two trees. Its legs rustled the brush as the spider scuttled into view. It stopped, its body less than ten feet from where they hid. At that moment, Weller hoped it wasn't intelligent enough to track footsteps. If so, their tracks would not go unnoticed.

Its mouthparts twitched, drooling venom and blood from the fangs. The song ended, leaving the forest in silence. Roman gritted his teeth in nervous suspense, as the phone delayed switching to the next track.

*Oh, you piece of junk, don't glitch on me now!*

A few more seconds of silence followed. The spider patted the ground with its legs, as though studying the terrain. The officers held their breath. In the corner of his eye, Weller noticed that Roman was tempted to run. He slowly tucked his hands under his chest and dug the toes of his boots into the ground, ready to spring up.

Weller mouthed to him, "No!"

The skin on Roman's face tightened as the muscles tensed. Those legs lifted and fell, gradually turning the spider in their direction.

*"And when I was just a little boy…"*

The spider flailed at the sudden blast of music, then eagerly scuttled in its direction. Roman quietly exhaled, his tension somewhat relieved. He watched the legs move in their circular motions, carrying the arachnid in the direction of the music. They could see it shifting to the left, then the right, uncertain where the music was coming from. It clawed at one of the nearby trees, then dug at the snow.

"Who else made it?" Weller whispered.

"I'm not sure. We all got separated in the chaos," Roman whispered. He watched the spider digging around the phone. "That won't keep it distracted forever. We're gonna have to make a break for it eventually."

"Yeah? Well don't go running off without me again. That would've been the second time…and it would've gotten us killed," Weller said.

Roman paused in silence as his mind comprehended the fact that he was now guilty of doing the very thing that he condemned Weller for all these years. He had left him for dead back at the lair, when in fact he was very much alive.

"Well, shit," he said to himself. He shuddered as he heard the spider fighting with tree branches. It almost appeared to be frustrated at the lack of prey. "Let's settle that later. Fact is, we can't wait here forever."

"Okay," Weller whispered. "We need a destination. Where do we go?"

"I honestly have no idea how far the main road is," Roman whispered. "We'll never get back to the cabins on foot."

"What about the vehicles?"

"I don't know," Roman said. "We haven't even reached the Calhoun Trail yet. It's almost a mile to the SUVs. I'm not sure we can make it that far with that thing on our ass the whole time. If only Stoll could've gotten us some snowmobiles or…"

They both glanced to each other, seeing the same look in the other's eyes. *The snowmobile!*

"It can't be far from here," Weller whispered. "If we can find the trail, we should be able to find it. All we need to do is locate our own tracks." Roman nodded. It was a simple plan. If they reached the trail and found no tracks, then all they had to do was turn north until they located their own tracks. With the storm having blown by, their trail would be intact.

They looked back to the spider. In the night, it looked like a giant shadow moving between the trees. That shadow was getting smaller and the rustling of trees was diminishing. It was moving away.

*Just another minute,* Weller thought. If it kept going for a few more minutes, there would be enough distance between it and them, as long as they moved cautiously.

Pine needles bristled behind them. The hairs on the back of Weller's neck stood on end. He heard the snapping of sticks and the sound of snow under feet. Obviously, it couldn't have been the spider, which was moving several yards away. That fear turned into mild excitement. It HAD to be one of the deputies. Weller looked back.

"McCarter?" he said. A gasp of air rushed into his throat. He saw the green eyes looking back at him. Seeing the urgency in Weller's body language, Roman turned around.

"Oh, shit!"

White snow sprinkled over the fur coat of a mountain lion. Its ears pointed up, displaying their white front, which contrasted sharply with the dark brown fur along its compact forehead. It had stopped the moment they turned. And for a long moment, they were in a standoff. It was a six-foot-long adult male, weighing at least two-hundred-forty pounds. It was not something anyone would want to tussle with.

Suddenly the air felt colder, and Weller remembered that winter was the prime hunting season for mountain lions.

"Good kitty," Weller whispered.

Its elbows bent, leaning its head low to the ground. At which time its slender, muscular body reared back. They noticed the tips of razor-sharp claws protruding from its paws.

Silence was no longer an option. Weller threw his hands out and shouted, "HEY! HEY! HEY!"

The mountain lion was not deterred. It sprang with both paws extended. Both officers jumped away, the lion passing between them. It crashed into the brush, wildly clawing the stems as it turned away. Weller aimed his Glock. As he squeezed the trigger, the cat leapt from the brush, unknowingly dodging the bullet. However, the large crack alerted it. It pounced to the right and then zigzagged behind a tree.

Roman fired a shot, the .45 caliber round striking against the trunk. He watched the tree intently, waiting for the cat to peek around.

"Look out!" Weller yelled. Roman glanced at him, then back to the tree, unsure of what he meant. It *was* behind the tree, wasn't it?

It was not. Using the cover of darkness, the mountain lion had moved several trees to the right. Roman saw its huge round eyes in his peripheral vision. He fired several shots wildly, one of them nicking its shoulder. The sudden streak of pain caused the cat to growl out. It jumped again to the side, this time running left and disappearing behind a cluster of trees.

A new chill ran down their spine as they heard heavy movement behind them. In the chaos, they didn't even notice the spider's approach until it was almost on top of them.

Roman whipped himself around and saw the huge legs expanding fifteen feet across. He drew his flashlight and shined it. The spider recoiled, covering its eyes with its legs. It only took a moment for its eyes to adapt and for the spider to advance. Roman emptied the rest of his magazine into it until the slide locked back.

"Come on!" Weller yelled, grabbing the Sergeant by the jacket and pulled him backward. They only accomplished a few steps before they were forced to another halt.

The mountain lion had leapt from its perched position in a nearby tree and landed directly in front of them. This time its lips were drawn back revealing long dagger-like teeth.

The drumming of feet continued behind the cops. Suddenly, the snarling jaws closed and those white ears turned flat, revealing the black fur on top. The lion was looking *up*, past the cops. With the arachnid almost on top of them, the cops darted to the left.

The mountain lion, apex predator of North America, growled and waved its claws at the huge threat. Only, this time it was defensively.

The spider reared up on its hind legs and hissed, the high-pitched sound introducing something the cat hadn't experienced since it was a cub: fear. It recoiled and swayed to its left side with the intention to retreat. But its agility was not fast enough to escape the four legs that swept over it like a lid over a chest. The lion snarled, scratched, and bit. Nails and teeth chipped against the rigid shell. It resorted to twisting and turning in hopes of breaking free. The legs swept it close to the mouth. The lion, in its struggle, tripped over its own feet, and the force of the jostling knocked it to its side.

It had no sooner hit the ground when the spider plunged into its shoulder. The cat let out a high-pitched scream, which diminished into a shaky exhale. It lay limp in the snow, froth soaping at the mouth as the spider initiated the process of cocooning.

********

"As if this wasn't hard enough! Like we didn't have enough goddamn problems!" Roman yelled out in frustration. Thick bushes and broken branches forced the cops to maneuver to the right then the left in a motion that induced dizziness. The mountain lion's echoes faded, leaving the forest silent yet again. Roman looked back. As he expected, the spider was out of sight. "You think it's done?"

"Hell no! Don't stop!" Weller said. It was partly directed at himself. His lungs felt as though they were about to explode from his chest. He was now coughing with each breath. He leaned and kicked his feet against the snow to avoid collision with a tree. The change in trajectory resulted in a repeat of that action to avoid running into another tree.

"WHOA!"

Weller yelled back. He staggered to the side to avoid colliding with the two figures that stood in his way. McCarter and Jameson stumbled back, arms thrown out in surprise.

"Holy sweet savior!" McCarter said. "We thought you were goners!"

"We?" Roman said. "I figured YOU got nabbed by that thing. Jameson, I was damn sure it had you."

"Don't freaking remind me," Jameson said. It was a memory that would haunt him for life. It was nothing but pure luck that he wasn't seized in those gigantic fangs.

"Where is it? Is it gone?" McCarter asked.

"It's just stopping off for an appetizer," Roman said, pointing his thumb behind him.

Somewhere behind their line of sight was the sound of an approaching body. Jameson stepped back, his face turning green.

"Oh, no, no, no…"

"Come on, let's get out of here," Roman said. "This way!"

# CHAPTER 19

The air hit them like a sheet of ice as the cops entered the Calhoun Trail.

"Golly!" McCarter said. "Which way is the damn thing?"

"No tracks," Weller said. "We were moving south, so it must be this way." They ran left down the center of the trail. The trees on both sides wrestled with the wind, as though a war of giants was taking place. The near high-pitched whistling made it difficult to listen for the spider. With no sight of it, it was unclear whether it was chasing them at all.

"There!" Roman said. They found the tracks left behind during their hike up the mound. They followed the tracks into the woods where they had found the snowmobile. They gathered around it and tilted it back on its skis. Roman popped the hood and brushed the snow from the engine.

Jameson took a step back and observed the damage. Both of the skis were bent up into a squiggly position. There were several dents and grooves along the side. What made him most nervous was that there were only two seats.

"Are we sure this thing will even carry all four of us?"

"You two will have to ride the side rails," Roman said as he cleared the snow away from the battery."

"Wha-? The side rails?" Jameson stood up straight, looking wide-eyed at the Sergeant.

"You're not sitting on my lap," Roman said.

"Yeah, but...side rails...?"

"Hey, if you'd rather walk..."

Jameson glanced at the trees around him, then out at the heavy snow along the trail. The logic became plain in his mind, considering the scenario they were faced with. A nervous smile creased his face. "Side rails will be great!"

"You think it'll even start?" Weller asked.

"It damn well better," Roman said. He opened the choke and turned the ignition. The engine sputtered once and died. Roman pounded the dash board. "Oh, you bastard prick. It's flooded."

"Great. Does that mean we're stuck out here?"

"No, you knucklehead. I just need to get back in there," Roman said. He popped the hood again and started working around the engine. He then perched on his knees, his eyes looking in the direction of a branch falling. The group waited in silence, weapons ready.

"I think it was just the wind," McCarter said.

"I'll feel better when we get down to that cabin," Weller said.

"Vehicles first," Roman said. He got back to work on the engine. "We need to warn Pino and Holt."

Weller sucked in a breath. In the turmoil of the creature's attack, they didn't realize that it was dragging two cocoons.

"They're gone," Weller said. All three officers looked at him.

"What?" McCarter said.

"It had them cocooned in its lair," Weller said. The recent memories made him feel sick to the stomach. "It captures you. Breaks you down with some sort of digestive fluid, then…" his voice trailed off. He didn't need to say anymore.

"Holy God," Jameson said.

"It's a spider," McCarter said. "It's a big-ass spider in winter! How the hell can it survive?"

"And how has nobody seen it?!" Jameson added.

"I don't know," Weller said. "It seems to only hunt at night. If I had to venture a guess, it eats a large amount then hibernates for a period of time. Again, I'm just guessing. All I know for sure is: it's no typical barn spider."

"What a shame," Roman muttered. "Then all we'd need is a giant boot!" He slammed the hood shut again. He turned the ignition and opened the choke. The engine groaned several times until it finally kicked on. Roman released the choke and increased the throttle to warm up the engine. "Voila."

"Oh, thank God," McCarter said.

Jameson was clapping. "Whoa! Alright. Let's get the hell outta…"

The Deputy lurched forward as an explosion of snow and brush ripped from the forest behind him. The branch holding the spider had collapsed under its weight, sending the enormous arachnid barreling to the forest floor. It rolled on its back, its legs curling repeatedly as though it were scratching the air.

"Holy fucking shit!" Jameson yelled.

"Gotta go!" Roman yelled out. He hopped onto the front seat, while Weller took the back. The two deputies stepped up onto the rail and held tight to the frame of the snowmobile. Weller reached out to each of them and grabbed them by the jackets.

Behind them, the spider rolled back onto its underside. Legs knifed at the snow and fangs reared back.

"GO! GO! GO!" Weller yelled.

Roman throttled the snowmobile and steered it out toward the trail. It launched like a missile, just out of reach of the spider's legs. The skis scraped against the debris along the ground, bouncing the snowmobile up a few inches.

As soon as they ripped out of the tree line, Roman veered sharply to the left to take the snowmobile northbound along the Calhoun Trail. McCarter yelled out as it tipped to the left, scraping his heels against snow.

The snowmobile leveled out. The snow sparred against the bent skis, causing the vehicle to move sluggishly.

The spider burst from the tree line and hissed. Legs vaulted overhead and ripped into the ground as the beast followed their trail.

# CHAPTER 20

Roman grunted and tilted his head side to side as the wind assaulted his face through the broken windshield. McCarter and Jameson gripped tightly to Weller's seat, hanging on for dear life. They saw the spider charging after them. Had the snowmobile not been damaged, it would have easily been able to outmaneuver the oversized arachnid. But the dents in the skis added some extra friction and the engine was continuing to sputter.

To make matters worse, Roman noticed that the fuel gauge was tilting further and further to the red. It had started with half a tank and already it was decreasing to one-quarter. It was apparent they had a leak.

"I can't see it!" Jameson called out.

"What?" Roman yelled through the wind.

"I CAN'T SEE IT ANYMORE!" Jameson yelled louder.

"Doesn't mean it's not there," Weller said.

"We're gonna be dead in the water if we don't find shelter," Roman said. He steered the snowmobile down a bend in the trail which led down a hill. As far as Roman could tell, they were going west, opposite of where they needed to go. "Ron, where does this path lead us?"

Weller observed the path, while using a hand to shield his eyes from the wind.

"I think…agh!" He squeezed his eyes shut as an icy burst of wind hit his face. "Uh…" he struggled to recall from memory… "It keeps going to the west and eventually snakes back to the north to the west end of the lake."

"Shit," Roman said. They couldn't wait that long. They would run out of fuel before they even got to the lake, much less the cabin, and thus be stranded again.

"We should've went to the main road!" McCarter said. "We could've turned at Boyer and gotten to our cars."

"They'd be snowed in, you knothead," Weller said. "We'd have better luck running on foot."

"We're not too far from that predicament," Roman called out. He looked to the right at the slope of the hill. There were several trees, but the ground seemed smooth enough to maneuver the snowmobile. He nudged Weller to get his attention. "Lake's that way, right?" Weller glanced to the northeast.

"Yes!"

"Alright! You county guys better hang on tight!"

"Wait, what the hell are you—Oh Jesus!" Jameson yelled. Roman veered the snowmobile off the path, brushing through the gap between two pines. Both McCarter and Jameson yelled out as the branches brushed against their backs like steel wool. The vehicle bounced up and down as it moved over the natural bumps and inclines along the terrain.

*Maybe it wasn't as flat as I thought*, Roman thought. He veered right, narrowly avoiding a head-on collision with a tree. Immediately he steered left again to avoid another.

McCarter and Jameson pressed their boots into the rail and clawed desperately to any part of the snowmobile they could. Snow sprayed in all directions, leaving a winding trail in their wake. The snowmobile bumped several inches after hitting a broken branch. Several pieces of wood flared into the air like brown sparks. The vehicle landed and started to fishtail. They had struck a sheet of ice.

"Watch it!" McCarter yelled.

"I swear if you don't shut up…" Roman growled. He wore a pained scowl on his face as he struggled to see through the wind.

"WATCH IT!" This time it was Weller. He pointed over Roman's shoulder. Ignoring the icy sting, Roman looked far ahead and saw the large mushroom shape shining in the headlights. It was the stump of a tree that had been cut down.

"Shhhhiiiitttt!" He steered to the right. The snowmobile rotated but could not get traction to go forward. Driven by momentum, it skidded on ice, its side now facing the obstruction. Roman cursed as he put it into full throttle. The snowmobile inched forward.

It struck the trunk along its back end, just behind McCarter's feet. The snowmobile went into a wild spin, throwing McCarter and Jameson to the sides. Roman's curses grew louder and more vulgar as he fought for control. That battle ended in defeat. The nose of the snowmobile smashed against a tree, the sudden stop causing Roman to faceplant on the dashboard.

Weller unfastened his belt and stood up, only to fall to the side from dizziness. He pushed himself to his feet and stumbled over to Roman. He unclipped his belt and pulled him off the snowmobile.

"I'm fine! I'm fine!" he said, spitting blood onto the snow. He stood up straight and rubbed his hand over his jaw. He winced as the nerves under a couple of cracked teeth lit up. "Where are the others?"

"I'm here!" McCarter called out. He limped on his left leg as he hurried toward them. His face was bruised and he was bleeding from his lower lip. He then stared at the crumpled front of the snowmobile. The engine groaned and clattered, as though it were a bucket of bolts. "I don't suppose we can fix this thing?"

Roman gave the snowmobile a quick look-over. The grill was smashed inward, as was the top of the hood. He tried to lift it up, but it had snagged on something he couldn't see. Smoke ripped out from the opening. Roman stepped back, waving his hand over his face. His nostrils filled with the smell of gas. The leak in the fuel tank had been widened in the crash.

"Nope, it's done. Best to stay away from it."

Jameson was stumbling toward them from twenty feet out. He turned his flashlight back on and waved the stream of light through the trees.

He turned and yelled out. Several arching appendages stretched toward him, all narrow and jagged in shape. The other officers became alert, ready to run. They saw Jameson fall on his rear, retreating desperately from the barren maple branches that rocked in the wind.

He stopped and sat in silence for several seconds, realizing it was only a tree. He glanced back at the others. "I'm never walking in the woods again!"

Normally, the others would laugh at him. But the reality was: they were all vowing the same thing in their minds.

"Which way's the cabin?" McCarter said.

"We're close," Weller said. "If we keep going this same direction, we should find the shore."

"Then let's get the hell out of here," Jameson said. He stood up and started to lead the charge.

Weller, Roman, and McCarter moved past the tree where the snowmobile had crashed and moved down the hill. He carefully watched McCarter's limp. The Deputy was clearly in pain as he walked.

"You alri—" His voice trailed off. He grabbed the flashlight from McCarter's belt and beamed it into the woods, toward the sound of scraping wood and snow. His eyes opened wide and he yelled out in horror. "Jameson! RUN! Look out!"

"I told you not to jo—" Jameson froze as he felt the vibrations beneath his feet. His frustration gave way to terror. He didn't even bother to look behind him to know that the spider was bearing down on him like a hawk on a rabbit. Jameson drew his Glock, only to have it flung out of his hand. The spider's outreached leg ripped his jacket, sending him barreling several feet down the hill.

The Deputy settled on his back, his head against the foot of a tree. He saw the legs vaulting high, each one appearing thin and narrow compared to the bulky mass that made up the spider's body. The pedipalps pulsed as though inflating with air. They arched up, rearing the two fangs back.

Jameson screamed as the spider closed the distance. He reached out frantically, grabbing for anything he could. His fingers found the tip of a branch and closed around them. He pulled up, only for the section of branch to snap, dropping him back into the snow.

Jameson yelled in hysterics and swung the branch like a baseball bat. It broke against the fangs, doing nothing to stop the arachnid. The legs curled around him. Screaming to the heavens, Jameson rolled to his stomach and wrapped both arms around the trunk of the tree. The claws struck his jacket, breaking through to the skin and pulled him away. He held on tight, despite the pain in his back and spine as the spider tried tugging him away from the tree.

Gunshots from the other officers did nothing to gain its attention. The spider stretched out a leg, completely baring the two curved talons at the end of its foot and brought it down like a hammer. The claw struck the back of Jameson's right arm just below the shoulder. His scream elevated to an ear-piercing squeal as the claw sliced through skin and muscle. The claw curved around the bone, ripping through tendons and bicep tissue. With a hard yank, the spider broke the bone, completely severing the arm.

Blood spurted in red swells from the stub protruding from his shoulder. With his grip on the tree broken, the other legs dragged the Deputy in reach of its jaws. His head listed back as he felt the fangs drop into the small of his back. His remaining arm scratched one last time at the snow before going limp.

"Move back!" Weller yelled at the others, warding them back with his arms out. As they retreated, the spider lifted itself from the Deputy and immediately began to bustle after them. They moved around the snowmobile and began to spread out.

The spider scampered its way to the tree, mere feet behind Weller. With his Glock loaded with his final magazine, he fired aimlessly behind him, hoping to land a lucky shot in its face. His heavy muck boots kicked up snow as he winded around the snowmobile. He turned and extended his Glock. The squeeze of the trigger resulted in a dull click. Seeing the partly locked-back slide of a jammed gun, he pulled back on the slide. The cartridge blocking the ejector port fell free.

The legs reached out like tentacle arms.

Weller screamed and fell back, wasting all remaining bullets as he fired aimlessly. Several of the bullets fell low, bombarding the snowmobile's side and hood. The bullets cut into its already damaged engine, causing sparks to fountain out from under it. The sparks spilled into the pool of gasoline below, sending the snowmobile ablaze.

Loud hisses penetrated the air, and the next thing Weller saw was part of the fire moving wildly into the night. The spider flailed, as two of its legs had been ignited by the flame. The sweltering flame illuminated its body as it tossed and turned in the distance.

"Good God Almighty!" McCarter said. He and Roman gathered around Weller and lifted him to his feet. They could see the spider darting back and forth in the distance, its movements marked by the flame. Its hisses continued as it thrashed about in the woods. The flame flickered behind the maze of trees, quickly becoming smaller.

They backed away from the burning snowmobile as the engine spewed sparks as large as lightbulbs.

"You think we killed it?" McCarter asked.

"I doubt it," Weller said. "I think we just pissed it off."

"You can count on that," Roman added. "Let's hurry up and get out of here!"

"What about Jameson?" McCarter asked. They ran to the fallen Deputy. The snow around him was red with his blood. His skin had paled, his face frozen with terror.

Roman shook his head. "He's gone. If we take him, we'll just slow ourselves down." They heard another screech beyond the darkness. "Come on! We've got to GO!"

McCarter gave one last look at Jameson, eager to make a plea for his friend's life. But beneath his emotions, he knew the Sergeant was right. He ran behind Roman and Weller as they made their way to the lake.

"I swear to God, if I come out of this alive, I'm squishing every goddamn bug I see from now on!"

# CHAPTER 21

The line of sight cleared as the officers burst from the edge of the forest near the shore of the lake. White streaks of moonlight reflected from the lake's icy surface. The sand and mud were hard as rock, frozen into various contorted shapes. Their feet rolled as Weller, Roman, and McCarter moved down the shore.

They could see lights a few hundred yards down. They were headlights from at least three vehicles, in addition to porchlights. As they approached, they could hear the rumbling of generators.

McCarter waved his flashlight, yelling "HEY! HEY! HEY!"

They could see Sheriff Stoll stepping out the front door. Two other officers came out with him and followed him through the front lawn. Hot vapor flowed from their mouths as the search team closed in on the cabin.

"Roman?!" Sheriff Stoll called out. "What the hell's going on out there? We tried radioing you!"

The group slowed down as they neared the garage. Gasping for breath, they fought against the exhaustion and marched for the cars.

"Sheriff!" Weller said. "Has anyone been around to plow the roads?" Stoll stated at him, dumbfounded by the question and absence of numerous officers.

"What? No," he said.

"Damn it!" Weller said. He turned to Roman. "That means we're stuck here. If we try to drive out on those snowed-over roads, we'll be sitting ducks."

"We're stuck between two shitty options," Roman said. He marched over to the Highway Patrol SUV. "Trooper! Pop the trunk! We need to load up!"

"What the hell's going on?!" Stoll yelled. "Where's the rest of your team?"

"They're all dead," McCarter said. "Or wishing they were." Stoll's bewilderment intensified.

"Dead?!" He looked around. "Deputy Jameson too? What the hell happened?!"

"It got him out in the woods about a quarter-mile westward," Roman said. He pulled an M4 Carbine out of the SUV. He gave it a brief inspection, checking the scope and ejector port then slammed home a fresh magazine and pulled back on the cocking mechanism.

Weller and McCarter got into the Sheriff's vehicle and pulled out a Remington shotgun and extra 9mm rounds for their Glocks.

"You fellas need to start making sense," Stoll said. "What do you mean, *IT*?"

Roman sighed, realizing he had previously been on the opposite side of this conversation, and how he felt when he first heard the very thing he was about to say to Stoll.

"Sheriff, after you hear what I'm gonna tell you, you're gonna think we're on drugs, but unfortunately we've got no time to beat around the bush," Roman said. "You've got yourself an overgrown spider in this forest and it's killing everything in it."

"A spi—WHAT?!" Stoll yelled.

"It's true, Sheriff!" Weller said. "It killed Pat. It killed Mark. Jameson, and Roman's troopers." He loaded several shells into the Remington and pumped the fore-end.

The trooper stepped forward, looking at Roman with questioning eyes. "What? Is he serious?"

"It's killing everything," Weller continued. "I don't know if it's stocking up for winter, or if it's preparing for hibernation, or where the hell it came from in the first place. But if it's still alive, then you can bet that it's coming for us as we speak."

The Deputy that had remained behind with Stoll burst into a fit of laughter. He leaned forward with his hands on his knees, his eyes squeezed shut and face red.

"Oh, man, you guys! The way you play it up so seriously…it's almost believable."

Roman grabbed him by the collar and shoved him against the side of the County Interceptor. The laughter came to an immediate end as the Deputy felt his back hit the door.

"How's *this* for believable?"

The Deputy was now alarmed and held his hands up.

"The hell are you doing?" Stoll yelled. Roman ignored him, keeping his eyes fixed on the Deputy.

"Deputy…tell me your name."

The thirty-something-year-old Deputy now trembled nervously, shocked by the strength Roman exhibited. He realized that the Sergeant wasn't kidding.

"Uh…Hilden," he muttered.

"Hilden, I suggest you stop your cackling and get your rifle out of your damn vehicle!" He released his grip. Deputy Hilden, no longer smiling, opened the trunk of the Police Interceptor and pulled out the shotgun.

Weller pumped his Remington and stood beside Roman. "You think these things will do any good against it?"

"They have a better chance than our pistols," he answered.

"Okay, I need some damn answers," Stoll said. "If you guys keep going on about a damn spider, I'll put in a formal notice for you all to be psychologically evaluated!"

Roman shook his head and walked off, irritated. Now he understood how Weller felt during the search for Deputy Pat. He noticed Stoll following him.

"Listen, Sheriff, you're gonna HAVE to believe us. If you don't, I'll have to detain you to keep you from running off and getting yourself killed."

Stoll stopped. His posture was now a defensive one. Weller marched past him to the cabin. "Good, looks like you've hooked up the generator. Have you called Headquarters? And where's everybody else?"

"I sent most of the units back to town almost an hour ago," Stoll said. "There wasn't gonna be much of an investigation till tomorrow, anyway."

"No, it's good," Weller said. "That thing had been stalking us during that time, so they should've been able to get out of here safely. Hopefully."

"Guys?!" McCarter said.

Stoll shook his head. He put a hand on Weller's shoulders in an attempt to pull him aside.

"I know you've had a stressful night but give me a break!"

"Stoll, this isn't a joke!"

"GUYS! Out there!" McCarter called out. He aimed a spotlight from the Interceptor window. A huge beam of white light stretched fifty feet past the garage. All eyes followed it.

The beam rested on the trees, then panned past the garage to the shore, forming a white circle on the snow covering the beach. The circle flickered as something huge passed by it. McCarter followed it with the light, catching the frolicking motion of legs as the arachnid disappeared into the trees.

Stoll stared, his confusion mixing with amazement. "The hell?" He was now questioning his own sanity.

"Son of a bitch, it's still alive!" Roman cursed.

"That settles it. We're not driving anywhere! Let's get inside and board this place up!" McCarter said.

"I say we get the hell out of here," the trooper said. He was pacing back and forth and looking hard into the trees. Initially, like Stoll and Hilden, he wasn't sure if he believed them. But now his heart was racing. Though he only caught a glimpse of whatever it was, its distorted shape was already engrained in his mind.

Roman saw the anxiety manifesting. The trooper was starting to inch toward the SUV. "Get inside, Trooper! That's an order!"

The trooper ignored the order. He had his own light fixed on the trees. The wind had gusted again, bringing the entire forest to life. A sharp whistle cut through the canopy, resembling a prolonged cat hiss. The branches twisted and turned, the ones from the leaf trees long and narrow.

He swept the light back and forth, continuously passing glances at the SUVs. The light moved past the garage. Like a giant claw, the legs curled in the light, blocking the spider's face as it scurried again out of sight.

A burst of adrenaline surged through his body. The trooper gave in to the fear and made a run for the SUV.

"Fuck this. I'm out of here!" he shouted.

"Trooper! We might need that vehicle!" Roman shouted. He started to sprint after him, but the trooper was already in the driver's seat. Roman reached out to grab him, only to retract his hands just in time to keep them from getting slammed in the car door. The engine roared and the trooper floored the accelerator. The tires spun, acting like buzz-saws against the snow. White powder soared into the air, spraying Roman in the face.

Finally, the tires got traction and the SUV took off. It bounced up and down as if surfing on the ocean. The snow bunched at the tires, slowing its speed drastically as the trooper tried to take it to the nearest road. Panting heavily, the trooper kept his eyes set on the path of the high beams.

He pressed his back to the seat and yelled as the giant body dropped onto the hood like an anvil. The spider heaved onto the moving object that concealed its prey. Its weight pressed the engine into the snow, its legs denting and clawing the metal on the top and sides. The rear of the car teetered up, causing the trooper to lean against the wheel. With his chest blaring the horn, the Trooper looked up into the windshield. Its fangs were scratching the glass, while the legs stroked the frame of the car.

The trooper threw his hands up and screamed.

Legs punched through the windshield like spears, shattering the sheet. Triangular shards protruding from the frame grazed against the exoskeleton as the legs reached in.

Snow kicked from Roman's boots as he tried to run after the vehicle. He was fifty feet from the tail lights when the spider sprang onto the hood. Roman pressed his rifle into his right shoulder and aimed to its head. He tapped the trigger repeatedly, putting several rounds into its carapace. The assault went unnoticed by the spider as it ripped into the interior of the SUV.

The trooper cried out as he felt the cut of curved claws shredding the meat behind his shoulders. Like a hook on a fish, they pulled him out through the windshield. Blood gushed through his uniform as his body slid against the glass shards.

Roman flipped the lever to full auto and bombarded the spider with bullets, which failed to penetrate its shell. The magazine emptied as the spider bit down on the trooper.

Roman jolted to the sound of a shotgun blast going off beside him. Weller pumped the fore-end and fired another shot at the arachnid.

"It's no good! Get inside!" Roman said. Weller pumped the shotgun and fired one last time before giving up and retreating to the cabin. McCarter, Hilden, and Stoll waited in the living room area, each sorting through weapons and ammo. Roman and Weller dashed in through the open door and shut it behind them.

"My God, I can't believe it," Stoll said. He held a tight grip on his Glock and leaned against the large rectangular window behind the couch. He could see the spider in the SUV's headlights. It was propped up on its legs, holding the trooper up horizontally, spinning him over and over again. He ran a hand over his sweaty brow, knocking his cowboy hat off. The spider was cocooning him as though he were a fly in a web.

Weller looked around at all the windows in the cabin. There were at least two in the kitchen, square shaped, with eighteen inches on each side. The one behind the couch was far bigger, being at least the length of the couch itself. If the spider could burst through the SUV windshield, it would have a field day with these windows.

They would not last long here.

"We're gonna need to come up with a plan and FAST," he said.

"Yeah, it doesn't look like we have too many options," McCarter said. "Even the rifle won't hurt the damn thing! If only we had a damn rocket launcher!"

"Sergeant Roman, what about the radio?" Stoll asked. "Can we get a SWAT unit in?"

Roman shrugged his shoulders. "I can give it a shot."

"Out here in the middle of nowhere? With the roads the way they are? It'll be forever before anyone gets here," Weller said.

"Corporal! I'd rather give it a shot than…"

"Sheriff!" Roman interrupted him. "He's right. We'll all be milkshakes in cocoons by the time anyone arrives. We're gonna have to come up with a plan ourselves. Unless one of you has a bazooka laying around somewhere?"

"Left it in my other pants," Weller remarked.

Sheriff Stoll moved back to the big window to observe the threat. His eyebrows scrunched together, his mouth slightly agape as he stared outside.

"It's gone," he said. Weller looked out through one of the kitchen windows. The headlights shined out on nothing but snow.

"Maybe it left?" Hilden said.

"No. It hasn't left," he said, backing away. "Everybody back away from the windows! Now!"

In one big stride, Hilden had moved from the couch to the back of the room. He inched to the side until he came to the stairway. With his eyes locked on the front door, he backed up the stairs past McCarter. He planted each step carefully, feeling that any sound he made would serve as a dinner bell. Not that the spider didn't know they were in there regardless.

He came to the top of the stairs and backed into the hall. A gust of air streamed through the bedroom on the left. He glanced through the open doorway, feeling increasingly unnerved by the sight of the broken window. He opened the door on the opposite side and moved into the guest bedroom. It was a similar layout as the other bedroom, with a back window positioned over the end of the bed. It was almost white from the reflection of the back-awning light. He sucked in several breaths before settling down.

"It's gone. It's gone. It's gone," he whispered to himself. He held his pistol close to his chest and listened intently.

The cabin settled into dead silence. Weller clicked off the kitchen lights to see through his own reflection in the window. The interior glowed a faint orange with only the corner light shining in from above the stairway. He stood near the stairway with the shotgun at his shoulder. Roman stood near the fireplace. He had a full magazine loaded into his Carbine. He stared through the large window with unblinking eyes, watching for any movement between the cabin and the lake.

The wind whistled, sending a draft in through the broken upstairs window. Then came the sounds of something dragging along the ground. Roman lifted the scope to his eyes, expecting the spider to appear outside the window at any moment. He trembled with anticipation, envisioning its ugly face peering in through the glass.

"Come on, take a peek," he whispered. He slipped his finger through the trigger guard, ready to shoot it in the eyes.

The right wall shuttered from a tremendous impact. Roman jumped to the interior of the room. He backed to the kitchen area with Weller and Stoll, keeping the muzzle of the rifle pointed at the fireplace. The wall shook again. The sound of groaning wood filled their ears, as though the planks were being pulled apart. Then came the scraping sound of legs clinging to the exterior. It sounded as though eight garden rakes were scuffing the outside wall.

The scraping quickly engulfed the entire wall. Gun barrels quivered as the cops maintained their composure.

"It's climbing the side," Weller muttered. McCarter, who had initially moved halfway up the steps, was gradually moving back down. He pictured the arachnid's overextended abdomen protruding from the side of the building, while its legs clung to the side like a bug on a tree.

Up in the guest bedroom, Hilden gulped as he felt the whole side of the cabin shake. The shakes were mild at first but quickly grew more intense. The window, originally black from the night air, was now brown as the spider's underbelly pressed against it. The awning light flickered from the other window. The walls creaked as the creature shifted. Suddenly, the light went dark.

Hilden yelped as he turned to run back into the hall. The glass shattered inward as one of the spider's brown legs lunged inside. The tip of the foot punched Hilden in the back, sending him stumbling into the doorframe. His head bounced against the frame, leaving him in a daze. The claw raked at the interior of the room, barely out of reach. Several other claws attacked the window, flaking bits of wood away.

"Come on!" Roman yelled. Footsteps pounded the stairs as he and McCarter worked their way up.

The Sergeant emerged in the doorway just in time to see the spider carve a hole around the window. Several claws pulled out at once, breaking away several slabs of wood. It shoved its head inside. Its face, as well as the two forward legs on its left side, were a mixture of brown and white from the burns it had suffered.

Those legs, the shell now crispy in appearance, unfolded like huge fingers. Hilden's alertness returned as the nerves along his ankles lit up. Roman grabbed him by the jacket and tried pulling him back. McCarter reached beside him and pulled on the Deputy as well.

Hilden kicked and flailed, screaming at those flicking fangs. He extended his pistol and blasted away, the bullets crunching between the eyes. One struck near the edge of one of the eye sacks, spilling a gooey fluid. The spider flailed with increased intensity, pressing the whole front section of its body into the room. Legs slashed like whips into the Deputy's midsection. Claws lacerated his stomach and abdomen, trailing intestines as they pulled away.

Hilden arched back, his scream now a dull groan as his innards were pulled free. Roman and McCarter continued to try and pull him away from its grasp on his leg.

The legs repeated their slashing motions, striking Hilden again in the midsection. Blood sprayed and bones snapped  The cops tugged again with all their might. Suddenly, they felt a release. Roman and McCarter fell back against the hallway wall, still clinging to Hilden.

"HOLY…." McCarter yelled. Hilden's torso slumped on the floor, with everything torn away from the waist down. McCarter stumbled back, nearly knocking Weller down the stairs in the process. Weller pushed through the crowd and stepped to the doorway.

The legs were in a wild frenzy, lashing out at the entire room. Chips of wood ripped through the area like sparks. The ceiling chipped and rained down from above. The hole in the wall widened as the spider tried squeezing its entire body inside.

Weller blasted the shotgun into the wild mass. He pumped and fired again.

"Look out!" Roman yelled. He grabbed Weller and yanked him back as the legs lashed at him through the doorway. He grunted as the shotgun was knocked from his grip. Claws ripped his jacket in a slashing motion, less than an inch away from his chest. Backed against the wall, they watched as the spider inched itself further into the room.

"Go!" Roman shoved him aside. They could hear its legs attacking the door frame as they ran downstairs. Weller jumped the last few steps and looked back. Two of the legs, one of them charred, scrabbled in the hallway. They marked up the walls and floor, splintering material before retracting into the room.

The cabin shook as the spider continued its demented assault on the upper floor.

"Can't stay here!" Stoll called out. "We need to run "

"You run, you die!" Weller said.

"Are you kidding me? This thing is tearing the place apart!" Stoll yelled, pointing up at the ceiling.

"It's trying to draw us out, Sheriff!" Weller said. "We can't outrun it!" The cabin shook again. Thrashing sounds reverberated through the ceiling as large portions of roof were torn away.

Stoll bit his lip, shaking his head back and forth as he watched the ceiling shake. Dust rained down as wood planks crunched overhead. He turned and moved to the door. Weller grabbed him by the back of his jacket.

"SHERIFF! DON'T!"

The shaking stopped, replaced by a distant drumming sound along the roof. The drumming turned to clawing, which moved down the left side of the cabin. The kitchen side window exploded inwards; the glass chased by the tip of a huge leg.

Stoll yelled out. He threw his hand back, dislodging Weller's grip on him, and ran out into the front yard.

It saw its prey darting through the porch light and into the snow. The spider withdrew its leg from the window. Its legs scrunched together, balancing on their tips and bending down. Then like a spring, they released, launching the spider over the porch.

The Sheriff could hear it turning along the roof, and in an instant, he regretted his choice to flee. In that moment, he turned around to double back, only making a single step before the outstretched mass came down on him. A brief scream broke the air as its abdomen slammed down on him like a pile driver. It touched down on his head, snapping it at the neck and driving it directly down between his shoulders. In that same instant, his legs and back snapped like tooth picks, and his ribs popped out of his sides like bristles as the spider's weight smashed him into the snow.

Weller watched through the window as fountains of blood spurted in all directions from Stoll's crushed body. It thrashed at the limp pile of meat with its legs, the jacket snagging on its claw. It picked at it like a child with veggies on a dinner plate, unsure if it wanted it or not.

Roman sucked in a breath as he watched the disgusting display. McCarter holding the shotgun from Hilden's car, stood in the kitchen and watched through the front facing window. Finally, the spider reared back as though it was about to encase Stoll in a cocoon.

Weller exchanged glances with the others.

"Any of you have a plan to get out—"

His sentence ended abruptly with the smashing of the window. The spider, having abandoned the corpse in favor of capturing the remaining prey, drove its head and front legs into the living room, ramming Weller like a bull. Weller reeled backward, his shoulders smashing down the bathroom door. He kicked the floor, scraping his boots on the hardwood as he backed into the space.

Legs swung from overhead and impaled the floor like pickaxes. The spider hissed violently, while clawing at anything it could to pull itself in deeper. Its abdomen teetered on the outside, sticking out like a cork in a wine bottle. The back legs kicked against the snow as the creature attempted to reach for the human.

Weller nudged himself back then rolled to his left. The foot of its leg hammered down in the space he had laid in an instant prior, rupturing the floor as it drove down. Weller scratched at the floor as he pulled himself into the back of the bathroom. The claws continued stretching toward them, their shells white and bristly.

Automatic gunfire pounded the air. The leg shook as the spider refocused its attack on the other humans in the cabin.

Roman held the trigger down, draining the magazine in seconds.

"YOU LIKE THAT, YOU OVERGROWN FLEA!"

Bullets chipped at its shell like chisels on rock. The spider angled its body to direct its efforts at him, crunching the edges of the window frame. Two of its legs curled in front of its face, instinctively protecting the eyes. Empty shells hit the floor as McCarter hit the legs with shotgun blasts. Pellets scratched the exoskeleton along the legs and bounced away. The Deputy fired again, only to discover that the weapon had run dry.

The two officers backed to the sink and switched to sidearms.

With the threat preoccupied, Weller ran out the bathroom door. His head was pounding with the repeated gunfire in the condensed area. He held his pistol toward the beast. He moved to the side to focus his shots on the area where the abdomen connected to the thorax. His boot came down on something, which rolled under him. Weller corrected his balance, realizing he had stepped on a piece of firewood. His eyes moved up to the fireplace, where several intact logs were stacked with a pile of newspaper.

He dove for the fireplace, stuffing the underside with paper. He grabbed the matches and lit the paper at several ends. The fire quickly spread and rose into the wood.

The gunshots stopped as both pistols ran dry.

"HOLY SHIT!" McCarter yelled in horror.

Weller stirred the logs, trying to get one to catch flame. "Come on! Come on!" Their edges glowed and a few flames appeared, but not large enough to pose a threat. Weller's eyes noticed the rack on the left side. He grabbed the fireplace shovel and shoved it inside, scraping up a flaming pile of paper. He twisted his body, hurtling it down on top of the arachnid's back. Hairs on the exoskeleton caught fire immediately. The spider hissed madly and raised high on its legs in alarm.

Its body flailed, knocking Weller back again. Twisting and turning, the spider pushed itself outside and scurried into the distance.

Roman caught his breath and pushed himself away from the sink. He could see the spider running along the lake, rolling over once as it battled the unfamiliar intruder on its back. The specks of orange danced like fireflies in the distance, quickly growing smaller until they vanished entirely.

"Goddamn! That shell is thick, but it lights up like a pile of dry leaves in fall!"

A gust of wind entered through the window, blowing snow into the living room area. McCarter sprinted across the room to help Weller maintain the fire. They stuffed more paper along the bottom, enlarging the flame. Finally, the logs were fully ablaze.

"This is all we have now," Weller said. "Bullets can't hurt it."

"Yeah, but how long can we keep it repelled with firewood?" Roman said. "If only we had a damn flamethrower! Or some damn napalm!"

"Sorry, *Rambo*, we'll just have to work with what we have."

"The fire clearly hurts it. If we keep hitting it with fire, perhaps we can inflict enough injuries to kill it," McCarter said.

"Problem with that is that we can't sustain the fire long enough to kill it," Roman said. "And this cozy little setup isn't gonna last the night. We'll be out of paper and wood in an hour, especially if we keep using it on the bastard."

McCarter shivered as another breeze hit his back. He knelt down and collected the fallen pieces of firewood. It was like counting ammo rounds. He placed one of the logs on the stack of newspaper to keep the sheets from scattering in the wind.

"Then we're gonna have to find a way to take the fight to it," he said. The thought of going outside, fully exposed to that thing made him shiver worse than the cold.

"That much is obvious," Roman said. "The question is, how the hell do we set that thing ablaze, and KEEP it ablaze. We can't spend all night throwing torches at it."

"We'll need to do something to keep it on fire," Weller said. He looked at the generator wires coming in through the door. "There's probably some gasoline in the shed. I saw the fuel drums in there before. There had to be some to fuel the generator."

"I see what you're thinking," Roman said. "Put some of that in a bucket and splash it on the prick, toss on a few of these logs...then we break out the marshmallows."

# CHAPTER 22

Orange flares danced from crackling wood, casting a twirling shine over the surrounding snow. With torches in hand, the three cops counted down then burst from the front door. Back-to-back, they looked around for any movement.

"I don't see it. You?" Weller asked.

"Not me," McCarter said.

"We waste any more time, we're bound to eventually," Roman said. "Let's get our asses to that garage."

Breaking their medieval-style formation, they shuffled through the thick snow to the garage. All three failed to keep their eyes off the ground as they passed Sheriff Stoll's mushed body. The blood had thickened in the cold, the body itself resembling a pie in a Sheriff's uniform.

Snow bunched at their shins with each step. They whipped themselves around, dragging flames along the air as they kept a lookout for the spider. They carefully moved across the front of the garage, ready to run in case the spider was waiting. But to their relief, it was empty, save for the various tools and the fuel drums.

The torches waved as the wind kicked up. Weller quickly turned and used his body to protect the flame.

"Hurry it up," he said.

"You'll need to wait outside," Roman said. "Only an idiot would play with gasoline with a flaming block of wood in his hand. McCarter, you're coming in with me." Roman handed his torch to Weller and moved toward the garage. McCarter looked around, unsure where to place his torch. With Weller holding one in each hand, he couldn't hand it off to him. It was time to practice a bit of resourcefulness. McCarter moved around the corner of the building and stuck the dry end of the torch into a compacted pile of snow. It stuck straight up, its tip blazing into the air like a big candle.

"Come on!" Roman called after him. McCarter spun on his heel and jogged into the garage. The cement floor was flat and even compared to walking on the snow. He moved to the back and helped Roman move the fuel drum around the owner's pickup truck. Weller stood on top of the busted door right outside, giving them light with the torches. They teetered the drum and rolled it along its edge, gritting teeth the whole way.

"Good God!" McCarter called out. The fuel drum felt as though it weighed a thousand pounds. "The owner must've just gotten it fueled up when he came for his winter getaway."

"I'd rather it be too full than empty," Roman grunted. They set the fuel drum down and he unscrewed the cap. "We need something to help us douse the spider. There's gotta be a bucket around here."

"There had to be a gas can or something for them to fill up the generator with it," Weller said.

"Unless it was full already...but you're still right. There's gotta be something around here," Roman said. They moved along the side of the garage, knocking over various tools and belongings. Roman got under the countertop and started rummaging through fishing items and power tools.

"Here!" McCarter called from the other side of the truck. He stood up straight and held up the large metal bucket.

"That'll do. Hurry it up."

McCarter was already halfway there when he spoke. He slammed the bucket down at the foot of the drum and leaned down to help Roman tilt it. Like pouring Kool-Aid from a pitcher, a stream of gasoline spilled from the opening and swirled into the bucket. It only took a few seconds for it to fill up.

"Okay, that'll do," Roman said. "Ron, any sign of that eight-legged bastard?"

"No!" Weller called over a gust of wind. He backed away and looked around for what seemed like the millionth time. To his great surprise, the spider was nowhere to be seen. He worried they would have struggled to even make it to the garage without being attacked. But so far, it was as if the spider had vacated the area.

Roman and McCarter stepped from the garage door. It was time to gather back in the cabin and set up their defensive position. Weller moved back to hand Roman back his torch. As though cemented to the earth, his left foot failed to lift as he tried to step. Weller fell forward, landing on his hands and knees. Fire and snow flared inches over the ground as the torches bounced from his grip.

The two cops quickly approached him.

"The hell's wrong with you?" Roman said. Weller tried standing up, only now, his leg was paralyzed up to his knee. He pulled at his leg with both hands, unable to wrench it from the ground. McCarter shined a flashlight down on it.

"Oh, shit!"

Light-brown strands of material clung to his boot and pant leg. Like a brachial artery, it broke off into several branches, each little arm clutching tight to its victim. Looking down at the snow underneath Weller, they saw the line of syrupy substance that stretched beyond the garage and cabin. It was a river of the spider's sap.

Weller grunted and cursed as he tugged on his leg.

"Son-of-a-bitch," he said. "The bastard set a damn trap!" McCarter reached down in an attempt to pull it loose. "Don't touch it!"

McCarter quickly retracted. Suddenly, the air felt full of menace. The feeling of being watched crept up along his back. He spun around with his flashlight in hand, anxiously wondering if the spider would come out from wherever it was hiding. There was no doubt that it was still around now. It was a matter of pure luck that all three of them hadn't been snagged in the sap. The wind kicked up again and hissed through the trees. Gasoline swished with each turn, dripping over the rim of the bucket and landing inches away from the fire.

"Put that down before you light us up!" Roman said, picking up the torches and moving them away. He got behind Weller and reached under his arms. He heaved back with Weller in tow. The leg was snagged tight, caught in the substance as though it were glue. McCarter got around them and helped to pull back.

There was a sticky sound, like Velcro pulling apart, as the leg slowly peeled back from the sticky trap. He was starting to come loose, albeit slowly. They tugged again with all of their strength. It was almost as if Weller had become one with the earth and would never part ways. The wind carried the numerous curse words that left their lungs.

"Damn!" Roman said after the fifth try. "This stuff doesn't want to let go!"

"We can probably use the fire and burn it away," Weller said.

"Yeah…and burn your leg off too. Not gonna help our current predicament," Roman said. He let go of the Corporal and started running for the garage. "Hang on! I saw a shitload of tools in there. There ought to be something we can use to cut you free." Waves of snow sprayed from under his boots onto the cement as he stumbled inside.

McCarter tried once more to peel Weller free. Pushing up with his knees, he failed to free Weller from the death grip of the adhesive.

"Shit," he muttered. He stood up and looked around again. There was still no sign of the spider. He looked up to the sky. The wind was bringing a new cloud front, which would block out the moon and coat them yet again in complete darkness.

He could hear Roman rummaging inside the garage. The fuel drum scraped against the cement floor as the Sergeant shoved it to the side. Tools clattered over the floor as he dug for anything sharp. He stood up, frustrated, as everything appeared to be tools for maintaining vehicle engines, likely intended for the boat.

There it was, the simplest tool of all. A fire ax was propped back in the corner behind the second fuel drum. He grabbed it by the handle and inspected the blade. Raising it high over his head like a lumberjack, he swung it down on the wood table. The blade punched through the two-inch slab almost effortlessly.

*Perfect.*

Outside, Weller pulled tirelessly at the snag. He kicked with his other foot, while clawing at the ground. His mind went back to when he and Deputy Pat were searching for Matt the plow truck driver, and the epoxy resin that was on that log. Little did he know at that time he had stumbled into a trap. And here he was again. Only this time, it wouldn't be as simple as removing a glove to escape.

"Hang on," McCarter said. "Roman's coming." Weller glanced back to the garage and saw the State Trooper running out with an ax in hand. In that moment he felt a sense of relief.

Then he noticed something above the entrance. The garage shuttered as though an earthquake was taking place. There was the scratchy sound of roof shingles being ripped away.

"SARGE!"

The spider scurried over the top of the garage, its abdomen swinging back and forth. The spider stopped at the front edge of the roof, its legs bent and ready to spring down at its prey. Glancing over his shoulder, Roman could see the tip of its fangs bulging from the fleshy pedipalps. Its body was twitching, ready to jump.

Being the nearest target, he knew its bound would be directed at him. In a heartbeat, he considered several different possible avenues of escape, all of which concluded with the knowledge he would not be able to outrun its leap.

In the corner of his eye, he saw the flickering of fire from McCarter's propped torch. A despairing yell escaped his lungs as he dove for the torch. He landed on his stomach and grabbed the piece of wood by its dry end.

In that same moment, the spider sprang. He heard its legs striking the ground on both sides of him as it landed. He rolled onto his back, seeing the flesh of the pedipalps peeling back to further expose those fangs. He thrust the torch upward into the jaws. Fire singed the soft flesh and bright orange flashes assaulted its eyes. The spider reared up and scurried backward. Its front legs brushed violently over its face as though it were removing an unwanted pest.

Suddenly, it darted in for another attack. Roman leaned up and waved the torch. The spider stopped in its tracks and clawed its legs at the air as if warding off an evil spirit. It hissed violently, inching more and more closely.

"Get the gas! Get the gas!" Roman yelled repeatedly. "NOW! NOW! NOW!"

McCarter bolted from his kneeled position and made a straight line for the bucket.

Through the numerous eyes stored in its membranes, the spider saw the prey running without the protection of the flaming hot weapon. The spider shifted its focus and darted for McCarter. Huge legs assaulted the ground as it ran, one of them blindly striking Roman across the face as it scampered past him. Blood streaked from his cheek and temple like laser blasts as he spun on his feet and fell. The torch hit the snow, burying its hot end a foot deep. Heat melted the snow to water, which then spilled over it, bringing the hot glow to an end.

McCarter grabbed up the bucket and turned, then screamed. Legs rose high over the spider's head as it sprawled over him. Legs swept across him, knocking the bucket upward from his hands. The gasoline ripped through the air in a glorious display, with nothing more than a few droplets hitting the spider. McCarter lunged to his right, avoiding its grab. Summoning all of his strength, he ran for the Sheriff's SUV.

The spider's feet rapidly pummeled the ground, its beating rhythm sounding as though numerous people were racing behind him. McCarter grabbed the handle of the driver's seat and yanked the door open. He threw himself inside, pulling the door shut behind him.

Shattering glass covered his lap as the spider threw itself onto the car. Claws squeaked over the metal frame, marking deep grooves all over the SUV. McCarter screamed, opening the center console and glove compartment in search of the keys, only to realize they were in Stoll's pants pocket. Clawed feet slammed down on the windshield, sending huge chunks of glass over the dashboard.

"Get out!" Weller yelled. He tugged desperately on his leg, unable to free himself from the creature's trap.

With legs coiled over the hood and side, the spider rocked the SUV back and forth. Through the smashing and groaning of metal, he heard McCarter screaming to the heavens.

McCarter scampered to the passenger seat in an attempt to get out the other door. He looked back, seeing the spider's fangs brush over the window frame, oozing venom like saliva. It was as if the spider was deliberately taunting him. He reached for the door handle and pulled it back. The latch popped and the door swung open.

Metal squeaked and groaned behind him. With his attention fixed on escape, he didn't notice the arachnid ripping the driver's side door away from the SUV. It reached in with its legs and tore at its prey. McCarter gagged and shouted as the curved cat-like claws hooked him through the back and shoulders. He threw his arms wildly, grabbing at everything he passed by as it pulled him out. Broken glass sliced his skin, spilling blood over the seats and snow.

He hit the ground on his stomach, his hands still flailing at his sides. His fingertips felt the cold hard metal of the severed door.

Grabbing its edge, he pulled it toward him and rolled to his back. The spider was mounted over him, its fangs directly above his chest. With one last desperate yell, he shoved the door upward at its face.

The spider slammed its jaws down. The door shook in his hands. Two pointed stakes punched through, peeling back tiny ripples of metal in the door around them. Venom continued to drip from their tips on to McCarter's chest. His arms quivered in the same exhausted manner as bench-pressing a dozen reps using two-hundred-pound weights. It was still trying to press its jaws into him.

Gritting his teeth in pain, McCarter locked his arms out to keep it off. The spider gradually applied the pressure. Tilting its enormous abdomen toward the sky, it tripled the pressure in less than a second. McCarter squealed as both elbows bent outward, snapping bone through the flaps of the skin. The fangs hammered down and plunged deep into his torso.

Weller pounded the ground helplessly, watching McCarter's body go limp underneath the spider. It was a mixture of fright and frustration, both pushed to the extreme. The arachnid lifted itself off its paralyzed prey and pried the door from its fangs. The door fell away and hit the snow. The arachnid repeatedly brushed its legs over its face and twitched its pedipalps.

Finally, it turned around and fixed its eyes on the target ensnared in its trap. Weller shrieked and pulled at his leg again. He threw his entire body backward, only managing to separate a couple of small strands of the resin.

The spider kept a gradual pace, saving energy in its approach. Weller grabbed his pistol and fired off a few rounds. Bullets hit against rock-hard exoskeleton and fragmented. The spider didn't even flinch.

Weller was close to hyperventilating. His mind flashed to that horrible lair and the bodies that melted in those cocoons. The thought of being dragged back, unable to flee, played havoc on his psyche. He could see the fading flames of the two torches Roman had set aside. Their flames were dying down, only rising an inch above blackened wood. Weller threw himself at them, stretching his arms as far as he could. His fingertips stopped an inch from the logs.

"NO! YOU BASTARDS!" he yelled. He jerked backward as a leg smashed down over the torches, killing what little flame remained. Weller kicked back, held firm by the trap. The spider reared its head back, exposing black fangs. Weller made his last stand, gripping the Glock with both hands...keeping the last bullet for himself.

Several shots cracked the air. The spider jolted as one of its eye sacks burst.

"You like that? You ugly prick! Here's some more!" Roman yelled. He squeezed the trigger of his Sig Saur, sending .45 Caliber rounds at the spider's face. The arachnid scurried backward, coiling its front legs over its face. It let out a tremendous hiss while lashing wildly at the air.

Roman staggered to his left, his face nearly torn open by the creature's claw. Two huge gashes marked the left side of his face from the temple to the chin. His ear had been split in two, with one side of it nearly dangling free. His facial expression was a combination of physical pain and personal rage. He fired another shot at the spider. The pistol cracked and the slide locked back. He had spent his last round.

The spider scurried to its right, its legs still coiled around the face. Then in one lightning fast motion, they expanded outward.

"Fuck."

Roman treaded backward as the spider scurried in his direction, dragging the huge abdomen across the snow. Roman threw the pistol, bouncing it off the spider's face. Snatching the fire ax from the ground, he turned and ran to the garage. Nearing the fuel drum, he raised the fire ax over his shoulder like a baseball bat and swung. The blade crashed through the barrel, spilling fuel all over the concrete.

The arachnid hissed and darted through the garage door, its abdomen stuck between the edge and the bed of the truck.

"Bastard!" Roman yelled. Dropping the ax to the side, he grabbed the drum with both hands. With barbarian strength, he lifted it up to his chest. Yelling like a man possessed, he heaved it at the arachnid. The barrel struck it in the face, spraying gasoline from its open end and the slit in its side. The spider scurried back, wrestling with the drum. Gas spilled over its head and thorax, then sprayed over the garage as flaying legs flung the heavy barrel through the windshield of the pickup truck. Glass exploded like shrapnel from a grenade, pelting the interior of the garage.

The spider charged the truck as if enraged, skidding its tires against the cement floor until it was pressed against the wall. Headlight and window glass peppered the floor before being knocked aside from the arachnid's feet. It turned, ready to charge freely at Roman.

The Sergeant turned to run, only to see that there was no back door to escape from. Out of bullets and with no way out, Roman grabbed several tools from the table and hurled them at the beast. It approached, dripping dark green blood from its ruptured eye-sack. Its fangs lifted, pointing their tips at him.

Roman snatched the ax from the floor and backed up as far as he could. It only took three steps for him to be pressed against the wall. Blood dripped from his face as he stared the spider down. He held the ax with both hands and cocked it back over his shoulder.

"Alright…you wanna dance?" Sucking in one last quick breath, Roman lunged forward, "LET'S DANCE!" He swung the ax forward. The blade struck deep into one of its pedipalps, spraying blood over the cement floor. Roman yanked it free and swung again, chipping the tip of one of its fangs.

The spider reared up, its front legs assaulting the ceiling in a fit of rage. It no longer thought of Roman as food, but as a threat. All four of its front legs slammed down on him at once, driving him down on his back. The ax hit the floor and snapped. Roman yelled, wildly throwing his fist up at the beast. He arched on his back in a world of pain as the four claws plunged into his torso. From the chest plate to the ribcage, curved nails at the legs sank several inches into his body and angled outward, as though opening a set of doors. Blood ripped into the garage in a grisly fountain as the claws opened Roman's body like a novel. Ribs and breastbone came out in huge slabs, exposing lungs, intestines, stomach tissue…and a rapidly beating heart.

The yelling came to a gradual stop as the spider began to lash at the insides, throwing them over the walls.

Weller closed his eyes after witnessing some of the blood splattering from the garage opening. The pained yelling came to a close, and the only thing to be heard other than his own frantic breathing were the flaying movements of the spider's continued assault.

He opened his eyes as the sounds came to a close. He could see the spider's abdomen protruding from the entrance, the legs twitching outward as though it was playing with Roman's corpse. After a few more seconds, it backed out, brushing against the pickup truck until it exited completely. It whirled around once more like a frisbee until it faced Weller.

The spider took a step, then another. Green streamed from its eye and jaws, while the rest of its face was covered in red. Dripping onto the snow along with the intermixed blood were droplets of gas. The odor was strong. The spider had been covered in fuel.

Weller tensed as he stared at the burnt torches, now laying useless in the snow. He was unable to free himself from the trap and had no way of lighting the fuel. He cursed himself for leaving his lighter in his other jacket, though it probably wouldn't have lit anyway. There was only one thing left to do.

He aimed his Glock and started firing off the rest of his rounds, each of them hitting nothing but shell. He ejected his mag, seeing that one round remained.

He stuck the muzzle into his mouth. No way was he going to go back to that pit.

*If I'm gonna die anyway…*

He squeezed his eyes shut and began to gently apply pressure to the trigger. The smell of gas filled his nose. A sharp hiss pierced the air. Whether from pure instinct, or the hesitation to take his own life, Weller opened his eyes. The spider's head was only a few meters away. He could see the gasoline rolling off its face in tiny rivers, trickling on the snow below it.

Memories flashed before his mind's eye.

*"You know what you should've done," Pat said, "is you should've siphoned out some gas, poured it onto the snow and lit it. Would've melted it right away."*

*"Yeah, smart," Weller said. "Take the gas out from the car…during a snowstorm, twenty miles from town. And you wonder why I don't let you do my taxes."*

*"Ouch."*

*"Besides, I'd be surprised if I could even get my lighter to spark in this cold."*

*Pat suddenly got excited.*

*"That's the good part actually," he said. "You don't use a lighter, you use a taser! I saw a video of an arrest. The perp's shirt was covered in lighter fluid from a cookout or something, and he tried to run. The cop got him with the taser, and whoosh…"*

Weller dropped the Glock and reached over his left hip, yanking the taser from its holster. The spider was over six feet away, its legs poised to scoop him into its fangs. He pointed the taser and aimed it at the arachnid's face.

A squeeze of the trigger sent the two barbs zipping into its shell. One plunged into the pedipalp, the other skidding over its forehead, zapping electrical charges.

The taser rattled several times as it pumped electricity into the spider. In the blink of an eye, the gasoline ignited into a massive flame that consumed the creature's face and back.

An ear-piercing hiss ripped through the night sky as the spider darted away in a frenzy. Burning legs carried its smoldering body back and forth. Running blind, the spider darted into the garage.

The fuel on the floor ignited, sending flames spreading up onto the truck and gas drum. The barrel exploded and launched like a meteor across the yard. In seconds, the entire garage was ablaze.

The back wall exploded apart. The spider, now entirely encased in fire, scurried into the woods. In pain and in panic, it scampered up the side of a tree, causing the branches to instantly catch fire. After climbing nine feet, the spider lost its grip and plummeted. It landed on its back, legs kicking below the burning branches.

It rocked back and forth until it was right side up. Another shriek pierced the air. The spider started to dart once again. Weller swallowed, realizing it was coming right for him. He leaned away and tried to turn, accidentally twisting his knee in the process. The pain never registered, as his mind was engrossed on the terror that approached.

The spider's speed slowed drastically. It began to rock side to side with each step. It stopped entirely, then stumbled another few steps until it was ten feet from Weller. He could feel the heat radiating from its body. The smell of gas was replaced by a ghastly smell of cooking meat.

Finally, the legs gave out from under it. The spider fell and rolled onto its back. Its legs coiled over its body in a deathly pose. The air was filled with the popping sounds from numerous ruptures in its shell as organs exploded and fluid bubbled.

Weller sat in the snow with clenched teeth, his body still tense from the horrific events that had taken place on this night. He glanced down at the taser then dropped it into the snow.

The wind drove the cloud front over the moon, eliminating the blue tinge of its rays, leaving Weller in the dark as he stared at the orange ball of flame.

# THE END

# CHECK OUT OTHER GREAT CRYPTID NOVELS

## BIGFOOT WAR
### by Eric S. Brown

Now a feature film from Origin Releasing. For the first time ever, all three core books of the Bigfoot War series have been collected into a single tome of Sasquatch Apocalypse horror. Remastered and reedited this book chronicles the original war between man and beast from the initial battles in Babblecreek through the apocalypse to the wastelands of a dark future world where Sasquatch reigns supreme and mankind struggles to survive. If you think you've experienced Bigfoot Horror before, think again. Bigfoot War sets the bar for the genre and will leave you praying that you never have to go into the woods again.

## CRYPTID ZOO
### by Gerry Griffiths

As a child, rare and unusual animals, especially cryptid creatures, always fascinated Carter Wilde.

Now that he's an eccentric billionaire and runs the largest conglomerate of high-tech companies all over the world, he can finally achieve his wildest dream of building the most incredible theme park ever conceived on the planet...CRYPTID ZOO.

Even though there have been apparent problems with the project, Wilde still decides to send some of his marketing employees and their families on a forced vacation to assess the theme park in preparation for Opening Day.

Nick Wells and his family are some of those chosen and are about to embark on what will become the most terror-filled weekend of their lives—praying they survive.

STEP RIGHT UP AND GET YOUR FREE PASS...

TO CRYPTID ZOO

# CHECK OUT OTHER GREAT CRYPTID NOVELS

## RETURN TO DYATLOV PASS
### by J.H. Moncrieff

In 1959, nine Russian students set off on a skiing expedition in the Ural Mountains. Their mutilated bodies were discovered weeks later. Their bizarre and unexplained deaths are one of the most enduring true mysteries of our time. Nearly sixty years later, podcast host Nat McPherson ventures into the same mountains with her team, determined to finally solve the mystery of the Dyatlov Pass incident. Her plans are thwarted on the first night, when two trackers from her group are brutally slaughtered. The team's guide, a superstitious man from a neighboring village, blames the killings on yetis, but no one believes him. As members of Nat's team die one by one, she must figure out if there's a murderer in their midst—or something even worse—before history repeats itself and her group becomes another casualty of the infamous Dead Mountain.

## DOVER DEMON
### by Hunter Shea

The Dover Demon is real...and it has returned In 1977, Sam Brogna and his friends came upon a terrifying, alien creature on a deserted country road. What they witnessed was so bizarre, so chilling, they swore their silence. But their lives were changed forever. Decades later, the town of Dover has been hit by a massive blizzard. Sam's son, Nicky, is drawn to search for the infamous cryptid, only to disappear into the bowels of a secret underground lair. The Dover Demon is far deadlier than anyone could have believed. And there are many of them. Can Sam and his reunited friends rescue Nicky and battle a race of creatures so powerful, so sinister, that history itself has been shaped by their secretive presence?

# CHECK OUT OTHER GREAT BIGFOOT NOVELS

## THE BEASTS OF STONECLAD MOUNTAIN
### by Gerry Griffiths

Clay Morgan is overjoyed when he is offered a place to live in a remote wilderness at the base of a notorious mountain. Locals say there are Bigfoot living high up in the dense mountainous forest. Clay is skeptic at first and thinks it's nothing more than tall tales.

But soon Clay becomes a believer when giant creatures invade his new home and snatch his baby boy, Casey.

Now, Clay and his wife, Mia, must rescue their son with the help of Clay's uncle and his dog, a journey up the foreboding mountain that will take them into an unimaginable world...straight into hell!

## BIGFOOT AWAKENED
### by Alex Laybourne

A weekend away with friends was supposed to be fun. One last chance for Jamie to blow off some steam before she leaves for college, but when the group make a wrong turn, fun is the last thing they find.

From the moment they pass through a small rural town they are being hunted by whatever abominations live in the woods.

Yet, as the beasts attack and the truth is revealed, they learn that despite everything, man still remains the most terrifying evil of them all.